# LIVING PICTURES

POLINA BARSKOVA

*Translated from the Russian by*
CATHERINE CIEPIELA

*Introduction by*
EUGENE OSTASHEVSKY

NEW YORK REVIEW BOOKS

*New York*

THIS IS A NEW YORK REVIEW BOOK
PUBLISHED BY THE NEW YORK REVIEW OF BOOKS
435 Hudson Street, New York, NY 10014
www.nyrb.com

The publication was effected under the auspices of the
Mikhail Prokhorov Foundation TRANSCRIPT
Programme to Support Translations of Russian Literature.

Originally published in the Russian language as *Živye kartiny* by Ivan Limbach,
Saint Petersburg, in 2014. All rights in the original text reserved by and controlled
through Suhrkamp Verlag Berlin.

Library of Congress Cataloging-in-Publication Data
Names: Barskova, Polina, author. | Ciepiela, Catherine, translator.
Title: Living pictures / by Polina Barskova; translated by Catherine Ciepiela.
Other titles: Zhivye kartiny. English
Description: New York: New York Review Books, [2022] | Series: New York Review
    Books classics
Identifiers: LCCN 2021050256 (print) | LCCN 2021050257 (ebook) | ISBN
    9781681376592 (paperback) | ISBN 9781681376608 (ebook)
Subjects: LCSH: World War, 1939–1945—Campaigns—Soviet Union—Fiction. | Saint
    Petersburg (Russia)—History—Siege, 1941–1944—Fiction. | LCGFT: Historical
    fiction. | Short stories.
Classification: LCC PG3479.R747 Z4813 2022 (print) | LCC PG3479.R747 (ebook) |
    DDC 891.73/5—dc23/eng/20211015
LC record available at https://lccn.loc.gov/2021050256
LC ebook record available at https://lccn.loc.gov/2021050257

ISBN 978-1-68137-659-2
Available as an electronic book; ISBN 978-1-68137-660-8

Printed in the United States of America on acid-free paper.
10 9 8 7 6 5 4 3 2 1

**NEW YORK REVIEW BOOKS**

CLASSICS

# LIVING PICTURES

POLINA BARSKOVA was born in Saint Petersburg, Russia, in 1976 and published her first poems when she was nine years old. She has lived in the United States since 1998. She studied classical philology in Saint Petersburg and Slavic studies at the University of California, Berkeley, where she now teaches. Apart from her work as a poet—she has published a dozen volumes of poetry since 1991, as well as several volumes of poetic essays— she dedicates her work as a literary scholar and editor to the poets of the siege of Leningrad.

CATHERINE CIEPIELA is a professor of Russian at Amherst College. She is the author of *The Same Solitude*, a nonfiction work about the epistolary romance between Marina Tsvetaeva and Boris Pasternak. She is the co-editor, with Honor Moore, of *The Stray Dog Cabaret* (published by NYRB Classics), and editor of *Relocations*, an anthology of contemporary Russian women poets.

EUGENE OSTASHEVSKY is an American poet born in Russia. His poetry collections include *The Feeling Sonnets* and *The Pirate Who Does Not Know the Value of Pi*. He is also the editor and main translator of Alexander Vvedensky's *An Invitation for Me to Think*. All three of these titles are published by NYRB Poets.

# CONTENTS

# INTRODUCTION

*Dying Pictures*

POLINA Barskova was born and brought up in Saint Petersburg when it was called Leningrad. Like all the children of that city—I was one—she grew up in the long shadow of the war, and especially of the *blokada*, the German siege that lasted from September 1941 to January 1944. How does a child grow up in the shadow of an event that had taken place decades earlier? A popular children's book for our generation was a photographic narrative of the siege that abounded in pictures of dead and starving people. Around the age of three I had thoughtfully scratched a swastika into the red seat of my wooden potty chair. By the age of eight I knew which war monument commemorated what. Across the street from my school there was a tiny preserved bomb shelter. The blockade was everywhere: in the missing buildings, in the walls still scarred by shell fragments, in commemorative inscriptions, in courtyard games. It was there naturally, as the background of the day, as the source of the day, for anyone growing up in that city at the end of the seventies.

One of Saint Petersburg's identifying symbols is the face of the Medusa that repeats on the neoclassical fence of the Summer Garden. The private sensation that an unspeakable horror had occurred here was covered over and reshaped by the mendacities of Soviet public remembrance. It was not individual suffering that the monuments commemorated but collective heroism, the harmony between the intrepid masses and their selfless leadership. Official discourse recast suffering as sacrifice, as voluntary contributions towards the purchase of victory. For whose sake? Naturally, for "our" sake. The state put itself down as the beneficiary of all attempts to remember, in order that any lack of obedience be framed as ingratitude towards those who died so that we may live. "No one is forgotten, nothing is forgotten," wrote the blockade poet Olga Berggolts, but the claim was more aspirational than factual. Uncontrolled private memory threatened to deprive suffering of the lofty purpose it bore in state myths. Left to its own devices, memory might dredge up the mistakes and crimes committed by the state before, during, and after the event.

The state had been completely unprepared for the attack. Officials in charge exhibited no interest in minimizing losses among soldiers or civilians. The police intensified political arrests and the arrests of Soviet Germans as the city was being encircled. Food was taken out of the city lest it fall to the enemy on surrender. Starvation rations for civilians contrasted with the relatively normal diet of the Party cadres. And after the war, in the so-called Leningrad Affair, the local bosses who did prevent the city from being taken were killed in a massive purge as Moscow reasserted control.

Private memory might connect the blockade to the class purges, to ethnic cleansing, to collectivization, to the Molotov-Ribbentrop Pact, to the war with Finland, to the gutting of the officer corps by Stalin, to the gulags, to the monumental violence of the whole Soviet experience. It might recall the deliberate starvation of two and a half million Soviet POWs in German custody, a Nazi crime encouraged by the Soviet refusal to sign the Geneva Convention of 1929. It might remember the deaths of more than seven million peasants in the Soviet famine of 1932 through 1933, centered in Ukraine, caused by forced collectivization and intensified by state refusal to provide aid. Private memory might put the blockade into Soviet context.

I am trying to explain why Barskova's book of short stories mixes personal reminiscence with stories about Leningrad writers and artists who lived and died in the siege. The author brings them back to life on the basis of letters and diaries. The second story, "The Forgiver," epitomizes the montage structure of *Living Pictures*. Barskova's personal memories intermingle with scenes involving survivors of the Holocaust and the blockade in a reflection on writing and the psychology of survival in general. This montage of historical fiction and autofiction persists throughout the book, switching sometimes between stories and sometimes inside them. Why is it that children and grandchildren of blockade survivors cannot keep the siege out of their lives, just as they cannot shield their personalities from being shaped by Soviet history? Why not let the dead bury the dead?

Historians of the blockade sometimes see it as a uniquely modern war crime. But it was a traditional city siege in modern dress. Inducing famine among civilians has always been the principal method of subduing fortified cities. Those citizens of Leningrad who still had Bibles could read about what was happening to them in the book of Lamentations, five poems bearing witness to the destruction of Jerusalem and the First Temple by Nebuchadnezzar: "the children and the sucklings swoon in the streets of the city," "the young children ask bread, and no man breaketh it unto them." The ancient poet lists the symptoms of what blockade medicine termed "alimentary dystrophy": "Their visage is blacker than a coal; they are not known in the streets: their skin cleaveth to their bones; it is withered, it is become like a stick." Perhaps the most haunting trope of the famine in the insistently feminized Jerusalem of the Lamentations is that of mothers eating their own children: "The hands of the pitiful women have sodden their own children: they were their meat in the destruction of the daughter of my people."

Stories of maternal cannibalism appear in other biblical sieges, no doubt as the most rhetorically effective expression of famine horrors. Josephus calls it "a deed for which there is no parallel" in his description of the savaging of Jerusalem and the Second Temple by the Romans under the noble Titus of Racine's *Bérénice* and Mozart's *La clemenza di Tito* (Josephus on dystrophy: "With dry eyes and grinning mouths those who were slow to die watched those whose end came sooner.") The Renaissance ethnographer Jean de Léry, in his account of the Catholic siege of the Huguenot city of Sancerre —famous today for its sauvignon blanc—avers to have been more terrified by Christian parents cooking their dead three-year-old daughter than by the eating of enemies which he had witnessed among the Tupinamba Indians of Brazil.

Perhaps it is to express the unnaturalness of the dystrophic body feeding upon itself that starvation narratives so often involve cannibalism, especially of children. In the period between December 1, 1941, and February 15, 1942, Leningrad authorities arrested a total of 866 people on charges related to the eating of dead bodies and even to the murder of the living with the intent to eat them. Some of this activity was said to be organized. The overwhelming majority of the accused were refugees from the countryside, largely women.

Did any of them commit the crimes they were charged with? One cannot trust accusations made by the Soviet police. Cannibalism was certainly more present in fear than in practice. Far more numerous were the murders carried out in order to steal food. My father's uncle is said to have been killed for a day's ration of bread.

There were gross and systemic inequalities in access to nutrition. The first to die were refugees from the countryside, who lacked residence permits and, therefore, ration cards. Ration cards divided citizens into industrial workers, office workers, and dependents. When food was scarcest, between November 20 and December 25, 1941, most civilians were allotted 125 grams of bread per day. Some people received a little extra at workplace cafeterias—more when the Party regarded their occupation as particularly valuable. Needless to say, Party officials valued their own labor the most. They rewarded themselves with meat. In December 1941, a pastry factory was pumping out baba au rhum for elite eaters. I have heard it argued that, if not for those imposed inequalities, no one in the city would have died of hunger.

The black market flourished. The starving would exchange all of their valuables for a handful of groats. By October 1, 1942, more than three thousand individuals had been arrested and tried for embezzlement or black marketeering. A military prosecutor reported that "the main contingent of those arrested for speculation and theft of socialist property are employees of the trade-supply organizations (retail, warehouses, bases, canteens). The main object of theft and speculation is food and other scarce and rationed goods." The attached list of confiscated valuables is impressive. Some of the perpetrators were making a fortune. Many of them were shot. The problem continued.

The winter of 1941–1942 was exceptionally cold. In January, the temperature fell to negative forty. Electricity did not work, nor heating. Water and sewage pipes burst. Public transport did not run. Apartment houses gaped like anatomical illustrations. The starving tottered slowly from house to house along streets choked in rubble, snowdrifts, and frozen garbage. Those who died in the street lay under ice and snow until defrosting in the spring. Of all the circles of the *Inferno*, Leningrad looked like the lowest—the ninth—whose sinners are frozen into the ice of Lake Cocytus.

Barskova is not only a poet and a writer of fiction but also a scholar of the literature and art of the blockade. She wants to know how people responded to and made sense of that kind of catastrophe, and what new artistic languages emerged to convey it. She also wants to know how people lived with one another in those conditions. The blockade proved a laboratory for extreme experiments in family life. Family members had to divide insufficient resources among themselves while face-to-face with each other's suffering. Sophie's choice situations were not uncommon.

*Living Pictures* subsumes the blockade under the more general theme of trauma. Whether set in the blockade or not, its stories focus on the cruelties people visit on each other in close coexistence, even on those they love. The author explores the long-term psychological effects of those cruelties on the survivors, who are then saddled with the task of forgiveness. It is hard to forgive those who are, like Hamlet's uncle, still possessed of those effects for which they did the murder.

Most of Barskova's protagonists had been the friends and

colleagues of the poet Daniil Kharms. Arrested on the charge of spreading defeatist rumors, Kharms feigned insanity to avoid the firing squad and starved to death in the prison asylum. His widow, Marina Malich (later Durnovo), appears in "Hair Sticks" and "Brothers and the Brothers Druskin." The philosopher Yakov Druskin rescued Kharms's archive and preserved his writings, as well as those of the poet Alexander Vvedensky, another victim of the Soviet police. Evgeny Shvarts, a playwright and children's author, worked with Kharms at the children's publishing house that also employed Vitaly Bianki, the protagonist of "Reaper of Leaves." Druskin and Shvarts survived the first winter. Bianki spent some days as a journalist in the city. The poet Berggolts was a prominent voice at the Leningrad Radio House throughout the siege; she appears in "Eaststrangement."

Dmitry Maximov, the literary scholar who secretly wrote poems about his siege experience, takes part in "The Forgiver." Barskova published his poems in *Written in the Dark*, her anthology of six blockade poets in translation. She also includes the poetry of the future science-fiction writer Gennady Gor and the painter Pavel Zaltsman. None of the poems in *Written in the Dark* was intended for publication: Soviet censors would never have given them the pass. Many were composed for no circulation at all, not even among the writers' closest intimates. The difference between the life they recorded and the life they were surrounded by was too great.

A kind of traumatic hypocrisy appears when what people say to others does not correspond to what they say to themselves. As a writer and scholar, Barskova is most interested in individuals leading a double life—in authors who created texts meant to be shown to everyone and texts meant to be shown to no one, whose private writings contradict their public writings. Her fiction commemorates Leningrad literature as a two-tongued, duplicitous literature, a literature with a false bottom. It is a literature whose central event is the blockade—the blockade flanked by NKVD purges.

The unofficial side of Leningrad literature came to light mainly at the end of the Soviet period. The poems in *Written in the Dark*, the earlier poetry of Daniil Kharms and Alexander Vvedensky, the philosophy of Leonid Lipavsky and Yakov Druskin, the prose of Lydia Ginzburg, the countless volumes of blockade diaries by writers and nonwriters—none of these was read by the authors' contemporaries, none had any effect on other literature of its time. Entering public life belatedly, these private writings of long ago remain strangely contemporary. We, the future readers for whom they were composed, have not yet absorbed what they have to tell us. We are absorbing it now, and *Living Pictures* shows the process of making the past ours.

A soft Stalinism is making a comeback in Russia today. The state has intensified its attacks on the remaining civil-society institutions, branding critical press outfits, human-rights NGOs, anticorruption centers, and even individual dissenters with the status of "foreign agents," whose activity may be declared "extremist" and punished. The authorities are targeting not only activists concerned with the future but also historians concerned with the past. Associations commemorating the victims of Stalinist purges have been forced to close. Led by former employees of the Soviet political police, the state is on a campaign to justify and idealize the activities of their Stalin-era predecessors. Exhibit A of the conservative nostalgia for Stalinism is the Soviet victory over Germany in World War II. Hence the official discourse around the war, and the blockade in particular, has returned to the mendacity and kitsch of the Soviet period. Serious historical or artistic investigation of the blockade has again become oppositional and subversive. This is why the blockade writings of Polina Barskova—as a poet, as a scholar, and now as an author of fiction—are still politically vital and ideologically relevant, unfortunately so.

—EUGENE OSTASHEVSKY

My blockade statistics and quotations were drawn from *Leningrad v osade: Sbornik dokumentov o geroicheskoi oborone Leningrada v gody Velikoi Otechestvennoi voiny*, ed. A. R. Dzeniskevich (Saint Petersburg: Liki Rossii, 1995). One million is a number usually given for total civilian deaths.

# LIVING PICTURES

# EASTSTRANGEMENT

> All a person had to do was say "death" or "victim," and
> they'd beat him mercilessly. The Germans let us know
> we were supposed to call the corpses *Figuren*, i.e. "mar-
> ionettes," "mannequins," or *Schmattes*, i.e. "rags."
> —from Claude Lanzmann's *Shoah*

THE TRAVELER differs from the non-traveler only in that
she chooses—to see. Sometimes, when you've just returned
from far-off places, you look around, amazed, and delay
switching off your traveler's vision; you notice that things
are the same but not quite the same in your familiar world.
A cup in the garbage drips an oily stream of coffee, and
something about this dripping grabs at your heart no less
than the sight of a statue, a beautiful woman, a viaduct. The
fish market on the corner emits an icy, end-of-day stench,
and it's as though you're briskly walking past death and
might, if you felt like it, say hello: I'm back.

Of course, it's not the urge to change places but the urge
to change times that overpowers us, drives us to get over our
fear and embarrassment about joining the herd: the airport
searches and disrobings, the water torture of the bus, the
centaur-like fusing with the limo. But once you're there, once
you get off the drug of your usual life and crawl out of your
snakeskin, a completely different experience of time awaits.

What new slowness takes over when traveling, and who knows what unexpected thing might happen? If you're lucky, a new trace, a new scar, will appear on your skin: You'll see something unforgettable, something that won't ever disappear.

(For my purposes, I'll call this "estrangement," a reckoning with my country. Now you laugh: It's *Eaststrangement*, an effect of my trip to the East and back to the great Western cities.)

## I. SURFACES

In Berlin the walls of buildings are covered with the acne of an old war's explosions and gunfire.

A pockmarked surface, whose texture makes you anxious. You want to plaster over, erase it. You want to smooth it out, restore it, and fix it up like new. Mainly, you want not to know. But Berlin's walls, like its squares, and doorsteps, and alleys... refuse forgetting. Berlin fights and claws and does not allow historical being, historical consciousness, to slumber.

I landed in Berlin after a short double visit to the city of Petersburg, where my professional obligations included showing the Leningrad blockade to American students—its commemoration, anguish, legacy, what have you. Meaning that I, we, were on a quest to part the curtains of time and enter its recesses without, of course, damaging anything.

It turned out the task was not so simple: Petersburg is no Berlin. This city has done everything to ward off, to cordon off, what happened here. The blockade is hidden; it seems to generate not so much new forms of discreetness as total muteness. (How depressed I was to learn that I've lived my life not knowing there's a monument to the blockade tram.)

The ponderous monument that greets people entering the city was dedicated, it turns out, not to the nominal event but to something completely different: Leningrad's designation as a Hero City. The walls of the small, perfectly *empty* underground museum are hung with ordinances, draped in frayed velvet. Later on, once I understood what a nasty dogfight they had over that designation, did I reflect that it truly deserved the decor! ...

Only after I and my twenty students, with their sharp young eyes, attentively studied the mosaic *panno* did we discover in one corner a chastely and, I would say, elegantly *wrapped* corpse—one of the "mummies." We also found in one of the display cases, among the weapons and attestations of military valor (and feeling a bit embarrassed in this company), a crumpled, blackened piece of blockade bread, which is not bread: It's the great ersatz life-or-death. This is how, when guests arrive and ring the doorbell, the host remembers at the last minute to shove the filthy boot or rag into a corner, out of sight. Likewise, this museum pushes out of sight the blockade body, the body of a human being, the body of bread, while earnestly, solicitously offering up euphemisms: *Figuren*, marionettes, medals, no people.

After our tour of the monument and the delights of blockade sublimity (the phrase belongs to Fadeev, who was expertly flown into the city and hastily evacuated in the spring), we decided to go to Victory Park, near the highway to Moscow.

Bumblebees were humming, children were shrieking, like they used to when Katya and I would go there. We walked and raced, we skated, we swung, we bought ice cream, it melted, our firm adolescent legs gleamed. We had no way of knowing the park was haunted, the forest was haunted, a forest from a terrifying folktale. As far as I remember (that's the big question, whether you forget something like that), no one ever mentioned how the park got its name, no one told us this was the place they unloaded and burned the weightless transparent glassy tender rigid bodies of the starving, the dystrophics: thousands and thousands and thousands of bodies. Some victory.

These days my sagacious interviewers love to ask me, Why and where did you get your blockade mania, your continual blahblahkade: Maybe you're avenging history for the grandparents you lost? No, it's nothing personal. The answer is clear! I'm sure that while Katya and I were twisting on our winged swings, and Katya's light-brown braid was flying into her mouth, on these same swings, flying along with us, were those somber blockade children, the ones who, in a 1942 documentary reel, were played by self-satisfied pink cupids/butterballs. As ten-year-olds we knew nothing about the blockade children. We never saw them, but they had to be somewhere: A million people can't just disappear. A million (the conservative, falsified estimate)—that's a lot of people.

What did I want to show my students in the park? The nothing? The emptiness? The well-maintained, lilac-filled garden? Me with my skinned knee escorted by a battalion of ghosts? I wanted to show them one of many possible answers to the question of why you can't escape the blockade in this city, though it's nowhere to be found. It's nowhere and everywhere, like a riddle in a folktale.

## 2. IN A SUBTERRANEAN VOICE

The Leningrad blockade is unfinished and infinite, it is not buried, the final word on it has not been said, but even so, what a multitude, what an absurd quantity of words it has produced! You could fill rooms, storage lockers of memory with the diaries alone...I've asked friends who are just as devoted to the subject, Where do I go, where do I find it, where is it now?

And my friend told me: The blockade is underground, it lives, it goes on under our feet, look for it there. My friend, my Cheshire cat: a sad, wry, colorful fairy out of Kosheverova's *Cinderella*, perhaps the most important film about the horrors of mid-century Leningrad (Shvarts quivers, Ranevskaia bares her teeth, the aging Zheimo sparkles). My fairy, showing me the next fruit, the next crossroad, in our ancient fairy tale, said: "Beneath the earth, it is hidden in a cave beneath the earth, there you shall find it."

Go to Akhmatova's courtyard. Go to the courtyard of Berggolts.

In the courtyard of Fountain House, where during the first weeks of the blockade Akhmatova for some reason still held out, they discovered *gaps*. I read about these gaps in a dozen blockade diaries but saw them for the first time that day in the museum in a photograph and felt terrified: A gap is an entrance to the underground, a living person goes underground to wait out death, but also to spend time in its company.

Having pried open and visited these gaps, Anna Andreyevna Akhmatova drew one step closer to her *Leningrad horror*. The gap was a test of nerves, a rehearsal. From there we proceeded to the next courtyard, the next blockade writer, the one who refused to evacuate, wanting to see everything with her own eyes, to taste/know it with her own mouth, and, it must be said, she tasted and knew.

To me, one of the most horrifying episodes in Berggolts's

fascinating diary was her false pregnancy: Berggolts (by this time having lost three children) believed she was pregnant from her blockade affair with Georgy "the Matador" Makogonenko.

Like most of her notions this was a fiction, but a deeply symbolic one: Berggolts, obsessed and shaken by the blockade, was not pregnant but sick with dystrophy, that is, she was pregnant with the blockade. We know all this from her blockade diary—one of the most vivid works we have from that vivid time.

Berggolts's diary, read together with her poetry meant for publication and her programs for blockade radio, constitutes possibly the fullest and most revealing body of writing about the psychological type (which type? Soviet, blockade, erased?) of an underground blockade person, whose poems and other rousing texts were broadcast almost every day on the radio—to the world and to the city. Well aware of the value and danger of her diary, Olga Fedorovna Berggolts hid it, buried it in the earth, each time she grew convinced they were coming for her. And they should have: The fact that they didn't touch her during Moscow's assault on blockade memory in 1946 can only be explained fatalistically—as a lapse on the part of the secret police, or one of their caprices.

Having shown my students the place where, underground, like a mysterious gleaming sword, a treasure lay, where an all-knowing diary was hidden, I, like the famed Pied Piper, led them onward—this time, to a church. How strange it turned out to be. I was welcomed by a priest with a tanned face and a placid gaze.

"I bid you welcome, please have your students come this way." I led my students past rosebushes, two Harley-Davidsons, and three cats, and we emerged in the territory of a mini-

museum, which took up no more space than my American
bathroom. Taking into account what the priest said about
his scavenging, I said to myself this was the best blockade
museum I'd seen in the city, though, truthfully, my compe-
tence at that point was fairly limited: to the shabby dusk of
the Rakovsky Museum on Soliany Alley, the empty galleries
of the City Museum where pages from Tanya Savicheva's
diary shone and burned on the walls, the two scrupulous
and enraged school exhibits with their (now the word becomes
appropriate) heroic curators. It's the emptiness surrounding
blockade memorials that pains me, and you can experience
that emptiness physically at Piskaryovskoe Cemetery. Not
a soul was there except for us; inappropriate, optimistic
Haydn was playing, and a squirrel dangled from a poppy
plant. Today the blockade seems to generate—instead of
compassion, attention, pity, collective mourning—an absence
of real, viable emotion: At the Holocaust memorial, the
entire square in Berlin was filled with people, but where are
the people who want to honor the victims of Leningrad?
And how do you assist those who want to honor them?

What did he show and tell us, our melancholy, sarcastic
priest? A sniper's empty brown bottle still inhabited by
spirits, miniature icons and crosses found on the dead, cas-
ings inscribed with names and dates of birth, a flask given
as a name-day gift (the recipient, they explained, was killed
on his name day). Imperishables: What couldn't decay lay
not so much in as over-across the ground of Leningrad starting in the fall of 1941, while millions [*sic*] of untrained and
unarmed soldiers kept laying themselves down into that
ground.

The priest and his friends travel to funerals to speak a
word of comfort in the miraculous event that a name is

discovered. He told us about those trips, his English was refined, a redheaded student sobbed loudly, kneeling at the altar, holding a cat on her knees. Empty ground stared at us from the photographs. There, over-across the ground, lie those whose brief military exertions—the length of a lightning bug's life—were deprived of any meaning by the monstrosities of Soviet military unprofessionalism, and who for so long, so very long, did not help the dying city, though they wanted to help, they marched to the front and ran to the attack: Some made it a hundred meters, some a little more.

## 3. MOTION

They ran and they walked, they crawled and they fell.

One time I had to describe how people moved during the blockade.

I confess I was unable to discover the right verb of motion. How did people move through the blockaded city during that deadly January: swollen, blinded, leaning on canes, passing by fellow human beings already turning into snow-drifts?

How do you take account of their method of moving along, when you're moving along a tour group of energetic young students?

"And now we approach the Philharmonic." What official blockade showcase could be more obvious: Here, in the summer of 1942, they performed the Seventh Symphony—basically, the piece of music most thoroughly explicated and celebrated by most of today's Petersburgers—the main event of blockade culture.

How do you convey or demonstrate (God forbid) to your listeners how the musicians moved in order to get here, many of whom were saved by this music in the literal, not the figurative, sense: They were given food so the Seventh would ring out over the city. How did the body (with a thick vest under the tuxedo, to hide the emaciation) move, how did the conductor Eliasberg's hands move, eaten away by scurvy?

What actually did move in the blockaded city, and what stood still?

With a metallic screech, the "American" tram raced across the bridges toward the Kirov factory, which during the blockade was ordered to produce a tank and rescue everyone, yes, everyone.

Riding along with us in the tram was a man who loved trams as though they were friendly beasts. One of the most remarkable people I met during those five days—though I suppose there could have been completely different remarkable people (seeing how many, of all sorts, I have met over these last ten years!).

Studying history, producing memory about a living city's historical disaster—this should be a personal, intimate pursuit: to each person his given place, words, recollections, ghosts.

But also: While there are witnesses alive and among us, there's still time to ask, to listen. Soon that no longer will be possible.

The storyteller on our blockade tram tour talked and talked, shuffled through photographs, looked out the window: "And there also were blockade trolleybuses," he exclaimed. "They had such bright colors," they were idled during the late and snowy autumn of 1941 and stood around "like Christmas trees, like bullfinches," people would get into them to rest for a bit and end up staying forever. The tram raced and thundered, drowning out his story about how you couldn't ride all the way to the factory and had to go the last distance on foot...

P.S.
Now I think we don't need, I don't need, to move around the city at all.

We need to enter the city and stand still.

And look for a long, long time. No need to rush anywhere. Look at the sky, the river, the restored walls, the grass, the Admiralty spire, whatever you like. If we were in Berlin, a city saturated with memory, I think they long ago would have hung on every building that escaped destruction photographs of these buildings as ruins, in their state of ruin. What more is there to say?

All this is the blockade, which has exploded and collapsed into Hades so many times, and which is now part of us forever.

# THE FORGIVER

I

MOUNDS of snow kept growing until they turned into white chickens. One shook itself off and turned out to be a tiny drunk holding a plastic bag. Sticking out of the bag was a geranium.

The drunk walked right up to the girl and stared into her face. This face, dripping wet, was made up as if to be visible to nearsighted patrons in the gallery of an opera house: enormous eyebrows, enormous lips, drooping dog eyes exaggerated by greasy black shadows. "You warm enough, honey? Waiting for your sweetheart, are you?" "Can I have some matches." "My wife kicked me out tonight. Quite a story, let me tell you." He belched and then whispered in a scary monotone, looking into nowhere: "Behold . . .

> Behold: the hawk prepares his strength:
> Now with beat of wounded wing,
> He'll swoop down, soundless, on the field
> To drink his fill of living blood . . . "

"Ha," she laughed, almost not surprised, "It's a real Greek chorus. May I have some matches? Would you please be so kind? Would you by any chance happen to have some?"

It was clear Father Frost would be moved only by excess politeness.

After three hours in the snow her matchbook had gone limp.

"Sorry, no, but take this flower."

Distracted, obedient, she grasped the bag filled with snow and walked off.

From the right, out of the bright, turbulent sky, one of Klodt's famous horses bore down on her, rearing its tensed body but already prepared to submit, malevolent.

2

While his latest sweet young thing was recovering herself, catching her breath, covered in a light sweat, the Professor, his forehead pressed against the windowpane, was trying hard to remember and then got it word for word (his exceptional memory!):

Not far from the stage, blocking the entrance, stood a man.

Taller than average, with a noticeable stoop, he kept his arms crossed over his chest.

He was strangely, even improperly dressed for the time, which was 1913, right before the war. He wore an impeccably clean white wool sweater: a skier just back from the slopes, the impression enhanced by his wind-blown look and slightly curly, vaguely reddish hair; his eyes were bright and glassy, like a bird's.

People walked past him, even grazing him in the crush, but no one suspected they were walking past Blok himself.

A famous photograph of the poet had informed all Russia what he looked like—an overexposed photograph: black curls, sensitive mouth, half-closed peering black eyes, the very image of a demon in his high-collared velvet jacket—but what matters is that this demon was copied from some recent opera!

The Professor liked to imagine Blok as the light-eyed, wind-blown, unrecognized changeling, and not as everyone expected him to look.

The Professor imagined himself such a changeling; no one really knew him or his true voice, and their not-knowing was his mainstay and his consolation.

3

The melancholy—the languor—the charm of the archive: the sensation of working a brainteaser, a mosaic, as though all these voices could make a single voice and yield a single meaning, and you could surface from this fog in which there is no past, no future, only guilty anguish. "No one is forgotten, nothing is forgotten"—no one can be helped, and everyone is forgotten.

Does that then make me Charon?

A late-night ferry in Petersburg, a flock of rowdy foreign

girls: "Can you take us?" "Can we have a ride?" "How drunk are you?" "Hey, come on"—cajoling, high-pitched chatter. We step onto the boat, and I notice near the captain's seat a bulging magnum, more like a jug. It's hard to do Charon's job sober: the souls keep up their lament.

The archivist ferries souls from one folder to another, from the type of folder where the voice never will be heard to the type where it might be heard by someone, at least for a while.

The reader herself becomes an archive so she can produce more readers. This is the physiology of it: You can't stop reading.

Sometimes it seemed the only way to get things read was to copy them out like Gogol's clerk, letter by letter, concentrating so hard that your tongue sticks out: like a cat's, or a boot's. To trace the fading scrawls and restore them, thus carrying into the present the very act of over-under-writing.

Word by word, declensions conjugations vanishing like lard and sugar in November. Commas and dashes blanch and collapse, stop making sense, can't breathe and melt away. Exclamation points were the first to die in blockade diaries, superfluous marks like those superfluous people, refugees without ration cards from Luga and Gatchina.

The main thing is to withstand time: time will do its best to crush you.

But the point of the whole exercise is to keep the other's time from permeating the time you carry inside yourself, for yourself.

4

And now another voice pushes its way to the front, rises to the top, arranges itself, and starts to recite.

Katya Lazareva, six years old in 1941, gray-eyed severe quick to laugh.

She and her mother would play a rhyming game. Mama would go first:

> There goes a bleary-eyed dystrophic,
> His basket holds a human buttock.

Then Katya would finish like this:

> The dystrophic's walking down the street.
> See how swollen are his feet.

Or this:

> The dystrophic reached the end of the wall:
> He sways and thinks: Now I'll surely fall.

And in the evenings they would play charades:

"First syllable: a poet with black curls, a sensitive mouth, half-open peering black eyes, the very image of a demon in his velvet jacket.

"Second syllable: Papa in his long nightshirt acts out a sinner whose demon-mama fries him in a pan."

The complete word was represented this way: a sled with a bucket of water and jars for rationed kasha being dragged by dystrophics staggering from weakness. BLOK-HADES.

## 5

Now here's another voice.

For his entire life the Italian Jew Primo Levi, with the zeal of a tactless noxious insect madman, wrote about the misfortune that befell him.

An embarrassed world literary establishment kept awarding him prizes and titles, which at that point, thank God, was not hard to do. Every time he got a prize, for half a year afterward he would digest it like a python and then disgorge another volume.

He never could write about anything else, or speak about anything else; he had dreams about it, went at his frail nondescript wife about it, and gave his interminably dying mother hysterics about it.

In his case proceeding from one book to the next meant magnifying the shot, refining the details:

> while being tortured the feeling is more "really, this
>     is what it's like"
> now it stank more than the two weeks of dysentery

Like all people endowed by nature and history with this timbre, he could not angle himself to catch time's racing current, so it pushed him out—and down the stairwell.

An embarrassed world literary establishment declared it an unfortunate event and accorded him yet another prize— for the speed and elegance of his fall, for liberating them all from his memories.

# 6

When they liberated the camp, the first thing he threw himself on was books, and these were his books: a textbook on gynecology, a French-German dictionary, an anthology titled *Magical Animal Tales*.

When he started writing his own books, his best friend—also, by the way, one of those who returned—hurled at him a word warm like a gob of spit: Forgiver!

In truth, Primo no longer wanted the death of those characters in his terrifying dreams, did not want revenge, did not want them led out and dragged to the scaffold.

He couldn't not think about them, couldn't not write about them, but he no longer had the strength to desire their beautiful, rightful demise.

Tales about magical animals—foxes, kites, jackals, and wolves.

# 7

His fleshy aging hands furiously grabbed the doors of the elevator. Father did not let them close, as though the elevator were an enormous seashell or a sea monster biting onto Andromeda's succulent body full of tender bits of gristle and dragging her down down to the bottom.

Never one to resist his own impulses, or to remember them afterward, Father now had to shriek his absurd condemnation through these doors, and that meant she had to hear and absorb what is best never incarnated in words.

Now he would say it, and her life would burn down, turn to rot, and go hollow.

And this hollow rotted vacated space would fill up with depression.

Once he had breathed out all his lines, she turned into sight itself; she looked into the face she knew as well as she knew her own, the face that was, in fact, her own:

enormous brows, enormous lips, dog eyes, perfect asymmetry—an overexposed photograph.

He was the secret everyone knew, a secret that interested no one but her and which lit up her shame from within.

"Secret": what you carry inside yourself.

In this sense she was now the secret of the elevator in the hotel October, and the raging old man was attempting to pry her out of this cherished position. A secret is what you carry inside yourself unseen, and all the while it is producing you, transforming you into something monstrous. A secret is radioactive.

## 8

The Professor always remembered these lines:

> She hoists her spider-zeppelins
> They float above the citizens
> They hang their heads above the land

And nets cast by the spider heads
Trace strange outlines overhead

How he loved his lullabies; in that dark fatal time they would swaddle-cuddle him like he was a baby ("spiders" were civil defense balloons) so he wouldn't up and lay hands on himself (and what do you know about suicide during the blockade? Thousands and thousands and thousands).

Those lullabies lived in him always, like a cancerous lump, like a fruit, like the pit of a fruit.

They would crowd around and press in on him, whether he was shaving, or lying and lying to his wife whenever he allowed a fresh new diligent student to touch him there, like that, and her dry pink scalp surged below like a clump of seaweed.

And the more he filled up on his little songs and longed for more, the better he understood he would never let them out.

The thought that his poems might crawl out of him and into someone's view entertained and repelled him.

Someone would get the idea they needed to understand or not understand them.

Someone would discern in them not their grotesque music nor their unclassifiable utterly individual forms and fossils, their crags and crevasses, but only the basic thing, stolen from time, which they lived through and which was frozen inside them.

And then people would see only the misprint, the mistake, the oddness, the wrong thing altogether.

"I have been writing poetry all my life. The volume titled

*Poems* came out in Switzerland under the pseudonym Ignaty Karamov. However, this edition, published without my supervision, abounds in crude errors and misprints. Suffice it to say that on page 23 two stanzas of the poem 'Insult' were reversed." The stanzas were reversed, the insult floods his vision, and through all of November and December, with its forked dragon tongue, it licks at the tender commas, the scrupulous exclamation marks, so that by January there's nothing left, as white as white could be.

# 9

And wasn't that the injury-insult and bag-and-baggage of that winter—that it still required burying: How cheerily the trucks ran along February's streets, collecting January's little bundles.

They called them "flower pickers" (corpses were wrapped in brightly colored sheets to make them visible against the snow).

The corpses were called "snowdrops" (for good reason—in anticipation of April's marvels).

A war correspondent there on a three-day assignment, fueling his writerly and quasi-ethnographic labors with American Spam, dedicated a special section of his notebook to the topic: SIEGE JOKES.

The fact was, during that winter they all looked like they were laughing. They bared their scurvy, bleeding gums. Smiling, dark-faced like monkeys, they—the dystrophics—made their way through the city.

The ones who survived put on weight far too quickly, grew bloated, introverted, and later, whenever they would meet, they were as silent as conspirators.

To speak or even think about that winter was forbidden.

That winter was their shared secret, as though they had performed an unnatural act.


## 10

"Ignaty Karamov"—what could be sweeter than to invent yourself from scratch?

To give yourself new hands, ears, eyeballs.

For example: cushiony white burning feminine strong papery hands, moist round eyes.

Above all a perfectly new soul with no cracks, no caries —just virginal blue enamel.

Ignaty Karamov does not know the crushing unceasing anguish of ivan ilyich doomed to keep on not dying aaaaaaaaah

But inside him the memory of what he was then, the shame of it, is always stinging, throbbing you lick the bowl clean weep scan the table howl lick again

Like all connoisseurs of pleasure, the Professor was craven and fragile. His pleasure was always full of little sounds—he had his own distinctive *kleine Musik*. Sighs, moans, whispers, feigned pleas and rebukes, unheard-of diminutive suffixes, shudders, astonished discoveries—all bubbles on the surface of his strange core motion, so easily thrown off.

He had a lizard neck and very languid, very dark eyes that went completely dead when he was coming and when he was leaving, trading one girl for another just as faceless and tender-mouthed.

Even his pupils rolled back.

To the poor anemic princesses who hovered around him, his sweet young things, he seemed at first to be a kind old man, but once they had attached themselves to him, once they had succumbed to his viscous icy fascination, they writhed and struggled, surrendering their vital warmth.

As he swallowed he would whisper—swallower to swallowed: "Behold: the hawk prepares his strength: / Now with beat of wounded wing, / He'll swoop down, soundless, on the wood / To drink his fill of living blood . . ."

Back then they would move on top of him like starfish anemones like tender seaweed in the tide back and forth back and forth

Then arthritis plated his bones like ice, and the move ment of starfish or any other kind of sea creature got more difficult.

## II

Those not privy to his secret were amazed by his popularity with young women.

After all, he moved like the Tin Woodman at the beginning of the story, before he was oiled, and his hands were starting to look like a falcon's talons.

He was as compelling as he was ludicrous: whether he was sharing with colleagues his shiny, newly acquired English or placing on the table, like trumps from a crudely marked deck, the names of the long-extinguished literary stars he was privileged to witness, all of them swallowed up by various abysses.

On the surface from the outside it was impossible to feel the magnetism of what was hidden inside him exerting its pull: inside was a Void filled with time, time's container.

## 12

To release them (the poems) would mean he forgave.

Like releasing and forgiving prisoners.

But whom should he forgive? The frozen city? The frozen century? The self frozen inside that century?

Forgiving took a whole lifetime.

Life became a suitcase that magically shrank in the process of packing: Other than the work of forgiving, nothing would fit into it. Forgiving somehow got strangely broken, twisted, and became almost a longing for the past.

I never could understand it—you have a professor with a crushed laurel wreath on his bald spot, affected, cowardly, someone everyone mocked, even his silly girls would smile whenever he . . .

And the whole time this frozen thing was living inside him:

Siege has cleaned our bowls,
And emptied out our souls,
Our grannies and our daughters
Are curled up into doughballs.

Forgiving is just that, forgiving, and it doesn't matter what episode you are unable to forgive, whether it is ordinary, private, and dingy, or on the scale of Bluebeard.

The mechanism is the same, and it is broken.

## 13

Can you release that blustery white night twenty years ago, when you definitively established that the person from whose head you were hatched, damp and pitiful, was not an interested party to your life?

That your past—which is to say, your future—spewed you from its mouth?

That by roaring, spitting into the elevator the words from the aria IL PADRE TUO!—he freed himself from them, from the name PADRE PADRE.

He'd given some thought to the freedom they sing all those songs about.

He doesn't show up for a meeting his own daughter asked for, having just lost her stepfather.

But as a consolation prize, divine providence sent down upon Nevsky Prospect a prompter-angel-geraniumphile— so you wouldn't do something stupid.

The waters of the Fontanka in winter are welcoming.

The work of forgiving crowded out love enjoyment recognition of the problem it crowded out language rather it consisted in the endless production of your own exclusive language.

A person engaged in the work of forgiving is monoglot.

## 14

"Memoirs of life in Leningrad during the siege, paradoxical as it may seem, have an aura of enchantment," wrote the engineer-optician, an observant disciplined person probably not inclined to self-deceiving fantasies.

On the same page of his diary, lower down, there is a detached account of the death of a girl, a neighbor, who was fired from her job in the fall of 1941 (the city was reserving ration cards, which went to workers), and who begged for food until the end, in vain.

So what was this enchantment? A kind of madness?

Spiritual "enchantment" (from "incantation," "chant") is the highest and most subtle way to flatter, that is, to deceive a person. In Russian Orthodoxy, it is defined as "the perversion of man's nature by the lie." A state of enchantment is present in the person who believes he has attained a high level of spiritual perfection to the point of personal sainthood. This state may be accompanied by the conviction that he is communing with angels or saints, that he is favored with visions, and even that he is capable of performing miracles. A person who has fallen into this state may be visited by "angels" or "saints," who are in fact demons feigning to be angels or saints. Moreover, the person in a state of spiritual enchantment may indeed have visions, but these are concocted by demons or are simply run-of-the-mill hallucinations. The spiritually enchanted person readily takes lies—lies instigated by the devil (the evil spirit)—for truth.

To the forgiver, "enchantment" is the power of the old abyss, the catastrophe, the darkness, to rule her life. In Russian there is no word for "survivor"—someone who survived, who came back.

I am attempting here to invent a word, to portray-convey such a creature, and more important, the process-means of living daily with the memory of what happened.

The forgiver attempts to shove words into the blackness, like shoving wads of paper into a wet boot.

The more words you can cram in there, into the dark, the gloom, the weaker the enchantment.

But these words go in and never come out: You feed the monster with them.

The forgiver-fanatic.

She takes her intricate fragile dreamlike abjection and turns it into a pamphlet.

How do you pick out a forgiver in a crowd?

The grave will repair the forgiver.

But a grave is a relative thing—some people never get the privilege, while for others, even in the grave, what an opportunity for spiritual growth.

There's a Po-Po for you—Edgar Allan.

Maximov—Zaltsman—Gor—Voltman—Spasskaya—Krandievskaya-Tolstaya—Gnedich...

How many like them were there, people who survived,

or somewhat survived, inside whom pulsed the shameful enchanting black lymph of secret poems.

From one perspective, it's not a big thing: A person has a whole entire life before after besides that little notebook—the shelf of publications, the four wives, the darting sparkling shoal of traitor-acolytes (*school of fish*), the dacha!

Even so, it must be said that you'll always know, and death agrees: There never was anything but that notebook.

That notebook is your cracked sediment, the only thing left of you—your forgiving.


## 15

I'll never have to say this to your face, so I'll say it this way.

Like I spoke to you on the phone once a year on February 4, when a broad deep impatient hearty voice would ask, how are things Po-Po-Po-lia? (As a rule he doesn't stammer, but occasionally he stammered.)

What kind of nickname is that? There is no such nickname.

And with no interest whatsoever in how I answered, he would start rumbling with poems—that didn't surprise me, either. Anything can happen in this world! There are Father Frosts Yury Gagarins there are BrezhnevLenins (up to age three I thought they were one person)

And that voice—like it was coming from Cocteau's scarlet flower.

The voice alone. So I'm telling you, Voice, I regret this is all true, I regret you did not have the imagination to come see me.

But that bright pink juicy twisting chunk of meat in the form of which your indifference lived inside me once upon a time is beginning to turn gray like a Petersburg morning it dies down and fades

Soon I will forgive you

# A GALLERY

PABLITO'S MORNING

THE DACHSHUND, and the duck, and the goat watched him protectively, and skeptically, from the cool shadowed caves of the room.

The blinding-white curtain rose and fell on a warm white wind, draping over the dachshund's torso each time so the animal resembled Little Longnose in an expensive peignoir.

His right eye refused to shut, the stuck eye of a contused doll.

"I'm lying here like an old doll, a bald baby with cracked paint peeling off."

When they pulled the curtain back and sun flooded the room he groaned and the duck turned away—from concern and embarrassment for him.

On a low bench next to the royal bed sat a woman. When she heard from the neighboring room ostentatiously hushed whispers and commotion containing a rhetorical question about the state of the sick man's health, she waved them away in disgust, Get out of here, just shut up. Observing the morning ritual, keeping watch over the body, was the pivot around which her life revolved: She sat up very straight.

Choice, they say, like I ever had a choice, since I was a child I've been consumed by your fiery fire your fiery dog that's all I've ever known

Ever since I was a child, like a fire brigade pushing a whipping hose into a house fire I've been thrusting into the dog's maw countless images all kinds of faces cities somebody's breasts knees ankles shanks profiles landscapes (cities seas countrysides) and very many women's bodies (flat-chested big-assed long-legged bodies with swollen genitalia and warts)

I kicked and dragged this throng over to feed the fiery demon like you take a virgin to the dragon every morning gag choke you monster. The monster would gag belch digest awhile and demand more that is completely new ones not like the previous ones.

The woman sitting straight-backed on the bench reached into a round red metal box and lit up a very bitter brown cigar. He started moaning again, this time from approval.

"Pablito, Pablito," she affectionately coughed out, "I just know this will pass and you'll get better."

This refrain usually had a magical effect on him, like the map of Treasure Island had on Jim Hawkins: for a minute the sky cleared, the curtain rising and falling. He stretched himself out, and his limbs, numb with morning depression, came back to life. He was very strong.

"Pablito!" shouted one of the players in his entourage, while swallowing a small, wrinkled *blood orange*. "You're so strong! Get a grip on yourself!" (Sounds of encouragement coming from this person were always sharp and definite, like a gunshot, or a fart.)

You are strong you are big you can do anything animals money women critics love you the sky loves you war your inspiration is infinite and will never run dry

Eres grande, eres poderoso, puedes alcanzar todo!

Tu es grand!

"You can do anything, you can. Tu es grand!" the woman chanted, keening a little, rocking slightly. With his left eye he watched her swaying head with that gray hair that sometimes descends on very young people like September frost. Somehow he always ended up looking younger and stronger than his young nurses and left them going gray with a litter of enormous infants, red from the Iberian sun as though they were sculpted from red clay.

But he never left his women in the morning.

Mornings he was needy and bereft, small, tender, blind. He required their incantations, their reassurances, their wispy palms caressing his face, soles, bald head. Now she'll start placing orange segments in his mouth, then, after blowing on it, she'll tip coffee into his mouth with a spoon. Sweet and bitter coffee. He'll groan again, turn onto his side, one leg, like a python, will slide into a Turkish slipper embroidered in black silk. Will thump the floor, despondent.

Ever since he was a child, hearing that demand—*get a grip on yourself*—he imagined enormous independently moving hand-tentacles lifting him up, caressing and embracing him. Disgusting!

With his opened left eye he sees yesterday evening's toll (in the morning you survey your nocturnal feats not without cringing)—a huge clay bowl with a centaur extending a cautious, exploratory penis over a contemptuous tart, and faint, delicate imprints—sun, sand, a dog, a severed head.

The head reminded him of the head of a recently deceased friend—he'd returned from the war with a hole opened by a bomb, he was always trying to display it, and he, Pablito, was always trying to avoid these demonstrations of the mysterious hole's contents. Though he also was curious, of course—about looking into the bloody bubbling crater.

Curiosity and the orange-eating hanger-on *did their work*— he reached for a pen and started scratching out on a piece of cardboard the image of a displeased dachshund: a rusty iron pen like he had as a child. Back then, precisely then, when for the first time he scratched out the profile of his severe aunt in a dozen variations (that's the key, variations on the same thing), flowing into one another like geological strata, chins and a huge gorgeous pockmarked nose, he experienced warmth, peace, the retreat of many-throated depression. Everything he had and made he rendered to depression—the throng of starstruck virgins, the pack of dogs, the gaping stinking wound under the stinking dressing on the poet's head, the thousand scribbled scenes—he couldn't not produce them, poor graphomane, everything they illustrated was consumed by the gray morning chill of nonexistence.

The dachshund, stoically refraining from attacking the thundering orange or precious slipper, told him about her fears in the night, how loud and alarming it got in the entryway, his entourage threatening to burst the corridor's intestine and spill out (or it would spill out anyway) into his morning room like Rabelais's tripe: "Tu es grand! Mommapoppa!"

He bared his teeth and growled (all the memoirs describe that doglike laugh) and threw himself into the fray with his minions. The goat Esmeralda couldn't keep up and broadcast her complaint.

## ON THOSE WHO WRECK SHIPS BY LURING THEM WITH FALSE LIGHTS

Describe the face of a woman howling, yes howling, in the plane's womblike dark.

Her swollen face and the swollen dark. The woman next to me, such a nice woman, with nice lines on her lips, exhausted from choking down her cries, disappears and returns with cognac. She raises the nip and, sobbing, uses the fire to stamp out the icy bubble, and hic-hic-hiccups.

The icy bubble, the aquarium. Smiling uncomfortably, he tells you the story of how he was given a useless but golden fish. The lovely captive was admired by all but breathed too much and too loudly.

He was, after all, incredibly sensitive: He sensed smelled everything understood everything saw and heard everything. He could hear the fish taking sharp, deep breaths during the night, trying to live, rising to the ceiling that divided water from air. He was exhausted by this breathing—and the fish was returned to the giver.

Here's what she thought about on the flight back.

In the course of our lives we meet people who do damage. Damage-people, people-cyclones, after an encounter you can only survey the remnants of your life, moving your lips mechanically, calculating the damage—a tree crashed through the (just repaired) roof, a dead wet bird with a twisted gray neck sprawls across the dining-room table covered in shards of glass.

For all that, they destroy to no benefit of their own, finding no tart sweetness in watching the other's house of cards collapse. Their abuse-amusement works obliquely, they don't enjoy ruining someone's life: the ruined life post-factum makes them feel shock, distaste, a chill down the spine.

Probably, though, there's something in their system that demands they destroy, they're powerless to deny this to themselves and they watch through the mist with the self-conscious irresistible smile of Erlkings waiting to startle riders in the night.

You can predict the approach of such people—like the approach of nasty, dangerous weather, a nor'easter.

Every time, right before the surprise encounter, the foreshadows/forerunners start up their distracting flashes, glimmers—now someone tosses out a word that's entirely and uniquely yours, a stranger in a bank drops a scarf with your gesture, and then the avalanche begins—keys and purse fall onto the wet floor, and it gets worse as it goes on (the sticky mounting humidity before the storm)—your name starts to flicker during casual conversations, and this whole process of approach, anticipation bursts like an abscess and the next encounter (exactly the same as all the previous ones) starts the countdown to catastrophe.

Afterwards your gentle loyal limpid patient angels float down descend arrive and find you in the condition of the unstuffed Scarecrow scattered everywhere

There there: the angel tucks a braid behind your ear.

She lifts carries you sets you on your feet makes you dance makes you exist.

This time you shake off the daze of nonbeing in a museum (and where have I not tried to compose myself—in a stadium, in a train station, on the bastions of the Peter and Paul Fortress, at the Berlin Zoo—in the enclosure for nocturnal animals...)

In the museum Turner breathes on you with a watery wave, knocks you down.

Transparent, full of sea and air, through which, like the scraps and cardboard of ballet scenery, his colors cast their glow on you: gold-ochre-gray-gray-black.

A battle of gold and gray, and all of it like lava, the main thing is that nothing is comprehensible, nothing fixed nor defined, everything changes and moves.

*The Wreckers*

The destroyers (the demolishers, the violators, the shipwreckers, the plunderers). The coast of Northumberland, in the distance a steamer is visible, either 1833 or 1834.

The catalogue links the painting to the following key words: stones / wind / danger / men / bandits / ships / steamer / castle / waves / shipwreck.

That's it exactly—stones-wind-danger, and in the bottom

right corner the ant-like swarm—the wreckers, those are people attracting all those steamers hoping the death cry will expel onto the shore useful tradable things.

He makes everything run together, you can't tell what or where, as though he were crying while painting. Or as though the person looking at all this—each person, every time—should look at it through tears. They live on! The legends live on about the wreckers from land who lure ships to their doom with false lights—to shallows and rocks, to destruction, to plunder, to winds, to danger.

The retired American navy officer John Viele dedicated his life to getting to the truth of these legends—in his tractatus he affirms that not only the lights but the legends about them were false.

A wrecker from the Bahamas, a gatherer of spoils from the sea, whom he interviewed, in answer to the question, "Do you set up lights at night?" said, laughing: What are you crazy we always extinguish lights at night *for a better chance*—the best decoy.

But there's also the legend that the village of Nags Head, North Carolina, got its name thanks to wreckers with their false lights. These wreckers hung their oil lamps on the necks of bulls (and sometimes broken-down nags) and slowly led them through the fog, along the edge of the tide, over the wet sand, thus maddening captains, boatswains, pilots, and ship's boys, who in their confusion ran their little boats into the shallows, straight into the arms of rapacious thieves.

P.S.
As we go through life, we ourselves find it necessary to do some damage.

The huge damp necks of bulls, the huge wet bodies of ships, the violet brown gaps in the mist, shouts, moans, curses, oaths—for what?

You keep walking along the sea, hoping that fate, the weather, will cast up a self for you: damp, fresh, newly born, and as strong as can be. But it always presses someone else's life on you.

You conscientiously pick through the wreckage, the flotsam, the rags and riches of the life you destroyed—no, we don't need this person's things, thank you very much.

Through ashamed angry tears you study the sweet slightly mustachioed face of your seatmate, and for the next ten hours of the flight you sleep on her stranger's shoulder, sniffling and shuddering.

GORKY IN LOWELL

*To Katia Kapovich*

I arrived in the city late in the evening during a snowstorm and collapsed onto the hotel bed to watch TV. On the screen were a pair of police officers (he a square-headed closemouthed widower with a buzz cut, she a frenzied Latina shooting with both hands), who conceded nothing to Arsène Lupin or D. with regard to analytical ability, pursuing maniac rapists along the muffled snowy streets of lower Manhattan. They solved each mind-bendingly complex and vicious crime in exactly twenty minutes. No matter how terribly things were going at minute six, fourteen minutes later justice and smarts would triumph—this was exactly what I needed, and I binged on five episodes.

Come morning the snow was still falling, and I walked through it along the empty canal to Memorial Auditorium. Men in cut-rate tuxedos and striking women-peacocks were trudging in the same direction. With good reason, since the instructions said we were to appear at the ceremony in clothes suitable for the occasion—your dry-cleaned, festive Sunday best. Ahead of me, across ice covered with what looked like soy sauce or brownish menstrual blood, tapped an elderly Puerto Rican beauty in a sequined emerald dress; she hesitated for a long time in front of a snowdrift, deciding whether to stick her heel in it. *Thrust it home, my angel!*—I swung back and forth behind her, trying to step into her fresh punches through the ice crust. As we processed into the auditorium, they sorted and separated us like human grain—relatives poured onto the balcony to take pictures, and the new converts were assigned to the orchestra, where they immediately began photographing the relatives who were photographing them from the balcony.

The master of ceremonies stepped onto the stage and told us, beaming, that the judge was late and not to be concerned. And we were not concerned. I read some of E. G. Etkind's classic text *Translation and Poetry*, where, having gotten access to Lozinsky's archive, Etkind uncovered "carefully copied out, and in a number of cases annotated, comments by Marx and Engels about Dante and his poem." I tried to imagine the plump torpid genius Lozinsky writing out these quotations on special note cards and with masochistic pleasure inserting them into a separate folder, and the skinny neurotic genius Etkind discovering and describing the folder with sadistic pleasure.

Amusing myself thus, I pulled some chocolate out of my purse, while my equally unconcerned Chinese neighbor sat without moving at all—not even when I dropped my book, my coat, or bits of chocolate on him. The wait dragged on for three hours, and several times some female officers came out onto the huge stage to do their tap dance: They danced awkwardly, missing steps, but at the moments of greatest rhythmic intensity never failed to shout, "Our congratulations, new citizens!" The waiting hall invariably exploded into a grateful ovation. Finally, the friendly tousled judge emerged onto the stage and ordered us to stand and take the oath.

"I, so-and-so, absolutely and entirely renounce and abjure all allegiance and fidelity to any foreign prince, potentate, state, or sovereignty," I enunciated with (so-and-so's) wooden lips.

Since for the time being, due to blissful diplomatic double-dealing, my former passport and right to visit my other country have not been taken away, the formula about rejecting my prince-sovereign was an airy figment, something like Lowell's canals, which had lost their direct reference a century ago—the formula was empty and broad, but whether it was that I got attached to it, or it got attached to me, I couldn't stop repeating this remarkable word:

abjure abjure

The judge suggested we congratulate our neighbors on our transformation the manikin and I turned—with our whole torso like wolves with their unbending necks—and looked at each other, since my Chinese friend wasn't about to smile or say a word, which I also thought was superfluous, we nodded at each other seriously, that's that, thus we mirrored each other and went our separate ways.

Putting into my pocket the paper flag on a splintery stick handed me by a gloomy schoolchild, and my certificate of naturalization, I went to get coffee. It seems I wasn't the only one with that idea, since the waitress eagerly asked me: "Did you get naturalized? So do you feel different?"

I smiled weakly and made an effort to say something inspiring, but she went on without waiting for an answer: "Now, when I got married for the first time, I kept asking myself: Okay, so what's different?"

She was about sixty and had that same rat's tail, that gray braid the writer Dostoyevsky couldn't resist.

I still had two hours before my train and had to kill them somehow. Typically I use a ruthless foolproof method—I head to the local art museum. Experience shows you can find a museum like that anywhere, in every town there's a morgue, a bank, and a museum, and in every museum there awaits a bent postcard, a faded (or just the opposite, completely dark) reproduction of some treasure.

Lowell couldn't possibly be an exception!

Past canals filled up with brown snowmelt, past rows of brick mills with boarded-up windows, past the tram tracks, I went in search of my museum. My path, however a mediocre sentimentalizing cliché this mnemonic shift may seem, was indistinguishable from my meanderings/musings along, say,

Obvodny Canal, say, in the direction of the Red Triangle factory, say, in late winter—that is, in May. When the moment came for me to walk by this factory for the last time, I gave in to my heart's impulse and went into the shop-salon where they were selling, what else, rubber boots and galoshes, but these had reproductions of paintings by the masters. Kramskoi's haughty, whorish unknown lady regarded you from her galosh, Kandinsky's eyeless peasants winked, van Gogh's terrifying windmills turned ... To resist the temptation was beyond human strength, and I had just about decided to acquire the landscape galoshes with the rust-colored mirrored pond by the high-spirited, high-living Levitan, when the shrieking and wailing of a Fury "don't try it on! you'll get it dirty! just buy it!" made me recoil and run back out to the frozen canal.

After several sessions of dialectical topography with the sleepy aborigines of Lowell I managed to identify the one old lady, walking a dachshund in a hat with a pompom, who possessed the secret of the museum—a pale-blue wooden building across from a parking lot. Having walked around it four times I thought I saw a functioning entrance and, jerking it open, startled a teenager sitting on the floor in headphones. She received her dollar, and I made a beeline for the permanent exhibit.

Said exhibit consisted of several depictions of Lowell in the era of its brawny youth and industrial might (in 1850 there were more looms clattering away there than in all of God's America), a pair of moonlit and murky landscapes from the brush of a locally produced success story (the poor fellow was so embarrassed by his association with burgeoning

Lowell and its clattering looms that his birth certificate lied that he was born in Saint Petersburg, Russia). The teenager humbly suggested I proceed to the second floor—to see the rest of our collection.

The second floor was unheated and very sunny.

The temporary exhibit. Along the walls blazed and floated and disintegrated paintings and photographs by the artist in his youth. Actually, the suicide never did manage to embrace anything but youth.

In his suicide note—even here playing up the persona of the exotic sufferer with poor English—Arshile Gorky wrote: "Goodbye my Loveds."

His name, of course, was not Arshile, and it certainly wasn't Gorky.

It turns out he had that name.

As I discovered that day, he had your name—only the second time in my life I met someone with that name.

Except that this time it was written in Latin letters, naturally, and the transcription from Armenian produced a somewhat different shape—a "g" at the end—but since I've carried that name inside me half my life, like a veteran carries a stinking slippery shard in his gut, I laughed at meeting it, this name, once more outside myself.

And it wasn't just the name: an unforgettable long face looked out at me from the photograph, I would even say a long-lasting face. When we first met I looked at you so much that you got nervous and asked to use my compact, and at the memorial service your father-in-law kept crying and exclaiming, "Such a face—he wasn't long for this earth, dammit!"

I thought a bit longer and realized it was your birthday: So let's celebrate.

(After you died, so I wouldn't lay hands on myself, my mother sent me to be watched by my strict and somber aunts, who lived on the banks of a Siberian river. I was nineteen years old, I had enough strength for ten lives and just as much fury at you for making me live those ten lives for nothing. I kept walking to the black August river to scream your name.)

Arshile Gorky's decision to become Gorky strikes me as a triumphantly failed strategy in the game of hide-and-seek that any emigration, any escape, represents—Ready or not, here I come. You have to do it—to take yourself a pseudonym as a pseudonym, a suggestive name ("Bitter") that is detrimental to carry through a world where it doesn't mean anything—gorrrki—the teenager rolled out, poking her head out from her headphones for a moment like a turtle, or a snail. No hint of arsenic to this appeal, nor any Marxist sympathy, nor the uncouth demand for the bride and groom to kiss and make it sweet. Like his eponymous predecessor, Arshile was a sentimental, infantile man who spent his whole life whimpering after his mother, who died of starvation during the Turkish games—his older sister was torn apart before the eyes of her impressionable son. All this, as we know, leaves an impression: Aside from repeated portraits of his mother, a wrinkled Niobe, his other masterpieces consist of nonfigurative bruises looking like fragments of female torsos, painted either from desire or satiety (artists' models, artists, journalists, actresses, female art historians left on his canvases here a slipper, there a paw, a breast—he found faces insipid).

His death, as often happens, was brought on by exhaustion.

Everything was going pretty well: an exhibit at MoMA, a friendship with Breton, the birth of black-headed (like beetles) daughters, whom he regularly renamed.

Everyone complained about him (his wives, his patronesses, their husbands), but they tolerated him, and he, in turn, tolerated them.

But one cold spring things started going wrong. First there was the diagnosis of colon cancer (from beneath the stage burst edifying tongues of hellfire and the chords of *Don Giovanni*), then the diagnosis was withdrawn, and the drunkenly celebrating child of fortune ended up in a car crash that destroyed his right hand and neck vertebrae. They erected a plaster brace on his neck and declared his hand immobile.

Pulling off his armor, with his healthy left hand Arshile Gorky loaded a different kind of brace and thus ended the phrase.

Here I must run for my train. Time to say goodbye. I looked for a long, long time (like you look at a movie screen) at the head of a bull, which you also could interpret as a tram. My mirroring return trip only reinforced my sensation that the abandoned factory blocks, the canals, the churches were too much to be real. While dreaming you can tell that you've dreamed this before and that you're also dreaming this very perception.

It's sweet to know: You know nothing, you know nothing about the future, but now you do know one thing about the future—you will never come back to this city.

# MODERN TALKING

THE DAY is littered with work.

In this warm dense thicket submerged specks of sunlight are blinking.

What is that?

That's you, all you, a you who reaches today's you only in flashes.

That's dove-gray blueberry bushes in a light seaworthy pine forest, a forest exposed, defenseless: someone took off its top (then dropped it, so it rolled away) like the lid on an aluminum milk can and filled it with cold light.

The blinding light washes over small bright insect-shaped berries. You find them by feel. By groping. They stick out like hard, shiny, cheerful ticks on a dog's belly. There are infinite amounts of berries here, blue-gray constellations receding into the dark underbrush. You grin at Tanya, your buddy in the junior Pioneer squad—at her blue lips, violet gums, purple tongue, teeth like black pearls. The squad's corpulent leader is grunting and crashing around in a raspberry bush. The raspberry bush pricks her vengefully as it defends itself. The leader's name is Hera. After her retreat, you, nurtured on ancient Greek myths, which the pedantic Kun shrank to unrecognizable flatness in his anthology for young readers, ingratiatingly and arrogantly (you mastered this combination at a young age) declare to her that Hera, they say, is the goddess of war. The mustachioed goddess is flattered, agitated.

Forty Panama hats sway among the blueberry bushes like a group of jellyfish on a sunlit wave.

In the hot grass of a clearing covered by the translucent fire of rosebay sits Andrey the grown-up. Who is he? I didn't know back then, and now he's completely gone—not a trace.

You can remember and forget at the same time.

Andrey the grown-up had wandered into the camp. A homeless man, an imbecile. They kept him around for a rainy day, for rainy work. To take out the garbage, to fix random things. He was sitting on the grass, squinting, shielding his eyes from the sun. The better to see you, my dear.

You don't remember his face, his voice, his shape, just the lavish awkwardness of your position. Everybody knows—the idiot hanging around the camp is in love with you. It's so endlessly awful that no one even thinks of teasing you. Everyone gets it. He follows at your heels, never takes his eyes off you. All around his island, along its foamy edge, Caliban, restless with desire, followed Miranda, occasionally offering his princess nice things: reeds, boughs, fluffy stalks to blow on. In return she taught him how to speak—she filled his thoughts with completely new words so he could more bitterly comprehend: She will never be yours.

Now Andrey the grown-up is terribly busy in the blueberry bushes. He strips berries from branches and pours them into your palm. The ritual: He feeds you, spoils you, and watches intently, soberly, possessively as you swallow them. If some berries spill out, he gathers them, crushing them in the process. You graciously wait and agonize.

You wave away the formidable mosquitoes of the Karelian isthmus. The eight-year-old sovereign of an imbecile. You don't remember his face or his shape. You vaguely remember he had curly hair. But not the same kind of curly hair as you, of course. Some sort of dry, colorless twists stuck up from his head. Whereas your locks were like burning plums. His were almost gray, dove-gray. He looked at yours in wonder. The wondrous Miranda. I remember the sensation of his wondering look. I remember his dirty palms full of crushed berries. I remember him following me like a shadow—I remember his shadow. In the blueberry bushes, on the scorching grass.

The berries fall to the ground, he gives a tortured smile. Then he points a finger in the direction of your hair—you benevolently explain in a child's bass: Curls. I have curls. To have curls is good luck (an embellishment of your weepy grandmother's). Obedient, servile, he picks up words after you as you go.

After parents' day, which cut the summer in two, a discotheque began shuddering in the Pioneer camp. The junior squad was allowed in for half an hour—to be shocked and thus distracted from the departure of their parents, who had brought their nervous offspring cherries and strawberries full of dysentery and nocturnal agonies. In the center of the discotheque stood a small television from which issued the celestial sounds of the musical group Modern Talking.

Small figures of indeterminate sex—hence the resemblance to Somov's marquises (curls, gold and silver, down to the waist, high-heeled crystal shoes)—are crying out: You're my heart you're my soul. In crystal countertenors the angels-castrati sang of the noblest things as they were showered, powdered, spurred onward by stardust, a flashing disco ball, cocaine frost. But I can see that only now: At the time, the eight-year-old pigmies and pigminnies, flowing in a controlled stream behind their leader, past their shaking and contorting older comrades, found it all strange and festive.

Eventually the small fry are shooed out of the club and into the deep July night, and Tanya and I wander back to our cabin in a state of enchantment. Andrey the grown-up, who, being a smelly creature, was not, it goes without saying, allowed into the discotheque, followed right behind us. He never let you out of his sight, your pathetic bodyguard. In the darkness you could hear him, "Curls, is it you? Curls, is it you?" Tanya is irritated by the senseless ecstatic repetition, she is preoccupied with some Ganymede from the senior squad, as she tries to impress on me in a hot whisper. You fail to understand her excitement but listen attentively, and only you find Andrey's shouts intelligible and reassuring ("And the watchmen draw out their cry, 'All clear!...'").

Thus he walked the perimeter of that summer, of the Pioneer camp's vigorous orphan life, your shepherd-Cerberus with the filthy disgusting hands. June, July, August.

Then, inevitably, the scene of disenchantment arrived. Some-one's vigilant parent on an unscheduled visit suddenly discovered the entire junior squad was infested, in the sense of lice and in the sense of Andrey the grown-up, who by this time had brazenly taken up residence in the corridor of the rickety gray cabin of the junior Pioneer squad on some unfolded cardboard boxes. A war on parasites was declared.

The cluck of icy scissors on the back of your head and a light tickly feeling—and your dead hair full of live creatures falls. Our leader Hera watched despondently as forty of her charges went bald. You exited onto the porch straight into the arms of your parents, who rushed to your side and kissed your tender new moon head and its tender new craters with curiosity.

Out of the corner of your eye you saw Andrey the grown-up's back withdrawing into depth perspective, saluted by a row of plaster Pioneer buglers cocking their horns. Then, as in every memoir that meets cinematic standards of bad taste, he slows down, turns around. He examines with distaste the new you, cleansed and distanced from lice and from him. Not-Curls and, as a consequence, not someone who is always lucky, who merits a wondering servile stare. This whole drama of a spell broken, of magic undone, takes place in a moment. You leave your squalid lodgings, clinging to your parents' little fingers—get me out of here, take me away from this clan of identical buglers back to the murmuring twilight city, the city of forgetting.

This is where they come from—the blueberry bush flooded with light, the stained palms, the berries spilling into a child's mouth, Curls is it you, your lice-infested locks landing on the floor with a thump, the pretenders' falsetto: *You're my heart, you're my soul*. The homeless man sniffs your flower-head burning under the sun's rays, you sniff his hands reeking of dog (recently, after a not particularly successful reading, a hoarse old man emoted: "I'm so moved that you use the word 'sniff' in your poems").

In these leftovers, these scraps you've managed to retrieve, there's no fear, no disgust, no meaning, no regret. Just something like bliss.

# ULIANOVA IN AUGUST

THE ACETATE dress, a dead and deadening silk, as though you had put on a plastic bag, and you're sweating so you smell like a little fox (that's what your squeamish stepfather used to say: My dear, you're smelling like a little fox again). Last year fate bestowed on me a dark blue one with polka dots, this year it was a tea-rose color with splashes of gouache and running watercolors.

Babushka, smacking her lips and breathless with emotion, hands Mama ten rubles, and you head for Child World to choose this summer's trophy. Dresses made of ghastly, suffocating materials arrayed on hangers beckon us with their little wings, give out a mournful rustling.

They hang there like larvae on the verge of hatching—Mama, a ragpicker-queen, a queen in exile, sorts through these marvels with her agile fastidious simian fingers and says disapprovingly, reproachful: Maybe this will do.

This was how Herodias, looking for a way to pass the evening, settled on a performance featuring dancers and the head of a grim foreigner. "Maybe this will do," she directed, frowning.

You released your gown from the iron rack it was stretched out on and, barely breathing, took it to the cashier. You went back to the apartment on Kropotkin Street and tried on the dress for your oohing and aahing babushka, your aunt, and your cousin, a somewhat strange teenager who initiated you into the pleasures of astronomy and botany, telling stories about the great explorers in the half dark of his dusty room. As he walked around the room and blared his commentaries, waving his unusually long arms, you lay there with your eyes squeezed shut from the intensity and occasionally asked him to pause so you could think over what he'd said; while thinking over what he'd said, you sometimes fell asleep, and he would sit there quietly and wait for you.

Then your other cousin would come by to see you, a glittering Harlequin, a swimmer (his stroke was the butterfly), and a smart aleck. He would grab your hand and you'd run DOWNTOWN, you couldn't keep up with him and he would laugh, while the other one stayed in his dusty room with botanical atlases propping up his virginal couch.

He stayed back there on Kropotkin Street, named for the geographer and revolutionary who on a Wednesday was reflecting-reporting on the existence of an ice age (sweating, spotted bald heads of academicians, debate, will there be any more questions) and by Thursday was packed off to the Fortress.

Each year you were allotted two new dresses: your school uniform and a second mysterious kind of dress for games, for dances in a twilight realm where no one could follow-find you.

## THE BUTTON

Finally only the last days of August were left—that sweet honeymoon stretch of summer whose sweetness is starting to turn sour; already you're running into schoolmates on the street, each bursting with the desire to tell you about her summer vacation without allowing you in—you, the advance guard of an enemy force of gray walls and activist school smocks.

But for now you're fine.

She was a dark-skinned girl with curly hair, vivacious and kind. There was something special about her serene, dark eyes and even gait.

How do you know that?

The library card was made of the cheapest paper, speckled with wood filings: In handwriting that slanted to the right (the ink was always running out, fading by the third letter), it listed one new treasure after another.

The librarian, a woman with the thematically relevant Basedow's disease, in a dutiful and hostile manner handed over more and more volumes—*Vladimir Ilyich's Childhood Years*, *How It Started*, *A Remarkable Year*, *Three Weeks of Calm*, *The Bullfinch*, *The Society of Clean Bowls*, *Lenin and the*

*Little Boy, An Encounter in the Forest, Lenin and the Night Watchman, A Mother's Heart, A Precious Name, How Aunt Theodosia Chatted with Lenin, How Lenin Gave Away a Fish,* Bonch-Bruevich, Krzhizhanovsky, Polezhaeva, Voskresenskaya, and, of course, you, my marvelous, anxious saffron-colored elf (you were gassed in the war), a coward and a traitor (you left behind your family and mad son in besieged Leningrad), as you walk, destitute, through a frightening market in an Eastern Republic while fleshy old women stare after your ruinous beauty. Are you buying or selling?

I greedily, squirrel-like, hoarded the books in my room and made my escape there, entering like a shadow into the welcoming rainbow-colored round dance, avoiding the shadows in my own home, the silent, despairing, bitter, transparent, fragile shadows.

"What a close family we were: We lived so amicably... In her physical appearance, Maria Alexandrovna was very beautiful—one sensed in her an immense moral force, self-possession, and integrity. Ilya Nikolaevich was very fortunate in his home life."

The march to the scaffold of their eldest son, who made a botched attempt on the tsar's life, was orchestrated by his gray-haired beauty of a mother like a Roman, impeccably: Steel yourself.

All this was thrillingly unrelated to my failed domestic twilight: my father and the cat sitting in a kitchen that smelled of the cat's boiled fish (occasionally, a codfish spine), waiting for my mother to come home, she was always delayed, life ticked by in the unbearable silence of expectation.

Meanwhile the Ulianov family was playing its games, loudly and cheerfully: "We always did things as a group." They would play scary monster, cowboys and Indians, hide-and-seek.

Why did you give your heart to her, of all the six perfectly blond perfect children?

Her closeness to her brother, almost a twin theme, though virtually nothing is known about her, just a casual reference to her sudden death in a typhoid ward. As your parents silently went to their separate rooms, you ran to put on that dress, and before the mirror the ritual of transformation took place: Olya/Aylo.

When they didn't have the energy for scary monster (and what kind of game was that?), the children kept a journal where they wrote down riddles:

> I sit on the threshold, shiny and round,
> Made of brass, or horn, or canvas, or glass,
> I hold one ear tight against the ground,
> And only allow the owner to pass!

My best dress, with a button at the waist—I'm riding on a sled with Volodya, no one compares to my cousin—he sails across the ice, focused and dangerous, a column of ice rises behind him like a tornado, and his sister's heart goes thump-thump.

# BROTHERS AND THE BROTHERS DRUSKIN

*A Tale of Annoyance*

M. S.: Are you asleep?
Ia. S.: Are you asleep?

THEIR TEMPERAMENTS WEREN'T COMPATIBLE

BEING brothers means, I suppose, having identical memories you can't share with anyone else. Nobody wants to share them, and nobody can. Mikhail and Yakov always remembered the same thing: They remembered a redheaded hot-tempered quick-witted fragile woman—their mother, a quite musical person, always whistling, humming, or making little sounds. "A barbaric organ," their father would tease, loving her with the kind of love from which there is no exit. After she died (damaging the brothers to differing degrees of intensity, meaning that for the one it was an earthquake of, say, a 4 on the Richter scale—cracks in the wall, broken glass, sawdust—while for the other it was an 8), he turned to rubble. I'm writing this in my rented apartment in San Francisco; there's a table explaining the Richter scale pinned above the garbage can.

What were they if not converging arteries of memory.

In their memory it's the beginning of summer. Dacha life: They would catch pollywogs and keep them in jars, and lizards, and crickets, and frogs. They would hold the frogs in their palms and stroke their bellies ballooning with terror; they weren't afraid of toads, though people said they gave you warts.

Deep into the dacha white night: They lie in their damp gray room and, exhausted, stare at each other like two malevolent owls. One has eyes that are green like gooseberries, the other's are brown like cherries. We've looked for so long at the very same things, we can't distinguish between the things themselves and the words we've said about them: We've told each other the same stories thousands of times.

The older brother gets up, goes to the table improvised from cardboard boxes, and begins writing. "Hey, what are you writing," the younger one sleepily grunts (capricious little prince). His eyelids are drooping, and the first and brightest clearest sweetest dream begins—the wallpaper pattern, tangled bouquets, withered bunches of leaves . . .

"I'm writing whatever I feel like." And the older one writes: dark depart daughter don't fret wed don't regret.

Annoyance is acknowledgment, it's the memory of shared fits of laughter. Annoyance is a kind of bonding. But it's also always a desire to get up, get out, run away.

To continue: The one was a dandy, the other an ascetic, one a voluptuary and a gourmand, the other saintly and celibate, and on it goes: smooth talker and stammerer, pedant and daydreamer, life of the party and wallflower, authority on Bach and authority on Bach. Brother and brother.

The younger brother, Mikhail, loved watching steamboats on the Neva (especially as they were leaving or approaching the dock), loved ballerinas (their icy polished extremities and mini-faces of royalty from a deck of cards), loved walking home on Nevsky Prospect at four in the morning (in general, he was fond of darkness), loved the smell of sweat from the hippodrome (the distinct smells of human and animal), loved the pause his teacher always took before dropping some unbelievable vulgarity and then, by means of a punning, macaronic alchemy, magnifying it kaleidoscopically in the twenty-six dialects at his command. (Twenty-six? Are you *serious*?) The younger brother loved when his name appeared above or below an article or review in a volume or a journal (his heart would give a light, satisfied knock), loved to turn on the radio and listen to lies and know they were lies, and to know that the lies themselves knew he recognized them, and continued to listen.

The older brother, Yakov, loved when a hangnail came off, or an eyelash-midge fell into his eye, or a filling came out—these were reliable signs that he existed, otherwise he wasn't entirely sure he did. All the humiliating requirements of existence—losing keys, knocking a lens out of your glasses, forgetting your briefcase and going back to get it (and doing this four times in a row)—seemed to him a legitimate penalty, a reassuring punishment for *something*, though it wasn't clear what.

The older one also loved to extremes his grotesque garrulous wizard-friends—arrogant, mannered, vicious, and completely unaware of him, aware of him only when he was making music.

When he sank his fingers into the harmonium, they would blossom and dissolve—like a beauty pampering her fingers in warm rich milk.

Once a girl with a distracted aristocratic face said, "I think

Yashka plays the piano better than Misha." "True," her companion agreed, "a lot better."

But the main reason they parted for good and lost all trace of each other was that Mikhail and Yasha loved the times in completely different ways.

Mikhail liked experiencing himself as something like a pimp for the era (pockmarked, with a gold-capped tooth and gleaming different-colored eyes)—he knew how repulsive it was, the era, but he also saw how entertaining it was, this era of his, and he expected it to drop rewards at his feet like a hunting dog. He was canny and cynical, at once extremely cowardly and extremely bold. He expected success from his era, expected victory in battle, "wanted it aaaaall." That extra Petersburg flourish.

Yakov would be appalled by the very suggestion that the era had any nonabstract nature. It was all gapingly, painfully clear: past present future. They did not touch, and he was the one charged with making sure they never touched.

When Yakov Druskin writes in his diary about the Leningrad siege, he writes like a perplexed, hapless scholar. You can't always tell he's writing about a deadly time—as though the diarist were observing it from far away, from above, from the outside. Or maybe the diarist can't actually see—maybe he's gone blind?

Yes, that's probably how it started, with their diverging sense of time, and later each had to decide how much interior space to assign to God. Yakov gave *almost* all of it, and Mikhail resettled God (he liked to salt his speech with *their* words) into Bach's room—a little crowded, but not too close for comfort. Mikhail just didn't let God into his own room. (Squeamishness? Selfishness? Shame?)

Simply put: Were they similar?

They weren't similar at all!

The one wore a bow tie and silver hat, and he would suck the traces of tar from his cigarette holder and speak in a moderate bass: that is, his voice was just deep enough to induce a ballerina to sink into it as if it were the Neva at its shallowest, four meters from shore, and to look around at him over her bony tanned shoulder—curly head filled with sand you're no goddess you're just a Leningrad babe he shouted at her what did you say she laughed, and when another took her place, he pasted the image of the finished one onto his memory like you paste a dot of gauze on a pimple sliced while shaving.

He would report to Sollertinsky on the changing of the ballerinas; Sollertinsky would throw open his window, lean out to see the new one, and laugh.

Such was the state of his healthy round heart and big clean lungs that it became clear he would never die (he died suddenly and horrifically before reaching fifty; you can hear the howl of protest in Shostakovich's telegram). But for now, Mikhail looks at Shostakovich with tears of happiness and envy.

The other brother sniffed ether to help prop up his broken-down existence before becoming a fifth-grade teacher in the backwoods; he'd completed three degrees in night school—philosophy, mathematics, pounding the keyboard—and mastered just about everything.

His voice was weak and papery, he chirped when he laughed—and yes, his fingers were long, as though someone had loosened a glove and let the clasp dangle sadly, anxiously.

So were they similar, or not? (Their mother would purposefully lay their glossy photos out on the table, like a game of patience.) See them look at each other—light mud-colored eyes gaze into red-brown eyes: grimaces, twitching eyelids, the mouth twisting to one side. One eye is narrower than the other: the asymmetry of resemblance. From the side, it looks like an actor rehearsing in front of a mirror.

Are they rehearsing themselves or each other? We look hard, and it becomes clear that one of the faces is a version of the other, a version of his *own* face's habit taken to its absolute.

Yakov, looking like an angel-orangutan.

Mikhail, looking like a person, an extraordinary fruit dripping juice, but then the wormhole closed up, and a drop of sap congealed there.

## FACEDOWN

Once Kharms said to Yakov while out on a walk, "You know, there's no way around it, your parents are going to die someday."

Yakov's eyes bulged out even more than usual, he made a sound like "ehhhh," shuffled his feet, and disappeared around the corner of Nadezhdinsky Street.

Kharms squinted like he was feeling dizzy.

He threw back his head, opened his eyes as wide as possible, and started watching the sky.

His eyes were the kind of blue you find only when you open a fresh tube of light blue watercolor paint made by the Leningrad factory.

"The coffin carrying the remains was transferred to the city in an open truck. The whole way his brother lay on the coffin, facedown. I was there holding him."

The brother writes the brother. The brother writes love. He tries to call back from the void a being with whom he spent most of his life in incomprehension. Mikhail strove for order, good form, celebrity, acclaim, possessions, meaning.

Yakov strove for renunciation, disappearance, deflected attention.

One of them wanted to live, the other wanted to not want to live.

The math teacher draws numbers on the board—his fingers are dry from chalk.

His teaching job is one step on the ascending path to invisibility.

There he will be saved, while everyone else, the visible ones, will expire in flames, filth, and ice.

It was the word "facedown" that sparked my comforting and painful (meaning, there is a kind of pain that arrives at the right time) desire to think about him—about Yakov Druskin, our champion and star student, our saint and our lamb, who rescued and made ready our paradise and our bestiary—

"Yasha Druskin lived with his bent old mother.

"She put a bowl of soup in front of him and said: 'This is for you. It's the last bowl.'

"He said: 'No, Mama. Give it to Marina, let her eat it.'

"His mother hesitated..."

Fifty-five years later, taking a drag on her cigarette, the Venezuelan exile Marina Durnovo added that the soup they gave her, she now realizes, was made from dog meat, but how it happened that she ended up giving Kharms's manuscripts to Druskin, she could not remember.

Yakov, you surrounded yourself with losers, people with heavy faces expelled from the times like children expelled from school.

Brother, did I know you?

The younger brother looks at the older before leaving the apartment—the ritual, as excruciating and prolonged as a toothache, of packing up and leaving behind.

Okay, let's just go.

## (THEN I WOULD LEAVE)

Blindly, hopelessly, and forever devoted to the great German composer Johann Sebastian Bach, the brothers, when they grew older, couldn't stand each other's playing.

"I never heard him play the piano after his graduation concert at the conservatory: he wouldn't play around me. When we studied Bach together, I would sit at the piano and he would sometimes pick out the vocal line, but the *ensemble* didn't work out—our temperaments weren't compatible. He went about forty years without a piano. At first he would come to my place to play (then I would leave)."

Brother, did I know you?

I would leave the room: At the time, I thought I was leaving because I was being tactful.

Later I thought it was from jealousy, or annoyance. Now I sometimes think it was from something more terrible—from indifference.

Mikhail, pursued by his brother's chords, that is, Bach's chords in his brother's interpretation and understanding (non-understanding!), with which he disagreed, would run down the stairs and out into the sun-blazed city. Petersburg's fog and gloom were invented by degenerate literary types, he thought to himself—anyone who's seen Smolny Cathedral in the April sun wouldn't dare write such trash. Mikhail took off, light and empty; Bach's chords, his own and not his brother's, filled him to bursting and drove him on. He ran through the city, getting as far as he could from the place, the moment, the action where the person who was the closest, the most intimately known, the most like him in the world, was professing something alien to him.

The prelude was alive in him like a fetus growing in a pregnant woman, twitching, smiling—and in order to hold it exactly like that, the younger brother vowed never to allow himself to hear his older brother's playing: tempestuous and instinctive. Mikhail ran all the way to Liteinyi Avenue and stopped to catch his breath, his mouth dry and salty.

# PERSEPHONE'S GROVE

*To Masha Rybakova*

> I drew my sword and sat on guard, preventing
> the spirits of the dead from coming near
> the blood, till I had met Tiresias.
> —Homer, *Odyssey*, Book XI
> (translated by Emily Wilson)

WHY DOES it have to be so complicated. Allusions anagrams nods winks confusion clichés? You could just tell the story straight: What happened, what made it happen. Tanya is telling me this, first lowering her gaze then directing it sharply at me, like a child's ball bouncing on a rubber string: Don't go there, you'll be destroyed—you should just write about it. What can I write, I tell her, there's nothing to write, nothing happened, as we know; how can you write about something that never happened? The Herzog tells a story in this regard, but it doesn't constitute a particular episode because it's impossible to narrate, meaning that it doesn't constitute a particular desire.

In San Francisco sparkles are mixed into the asphalt. Under your feet the celestial night sphere flashes and creaks, dirtied and defiled by the leavings of existence. Rats, Queens of the Night, squeal in their signature coloratura soprano, urging you on to vengeance and world domination. I watched those flashes as I walked hand in hand with my betrothed along the dark alleys of the Tenderloin. It was one of those rare acute moments when holding hands, shaking hands, means something, and you know it means more than one thing. The asphalt glittered and trembled under our feet, and I was able to keep walking only by holding on to you.

The starry sky underfoot and the breaking of all moral codes—that was my purpose then, but this time...

This time: As I descended into the Montgomery metro station, right there on the steps a man was squatting and defecating, his buttocks proudly and ominously purple in the darkness.

He felt himself completely free, but I was somehow embarrassed by this changeling of the "public-private" and retreated, deciding to try my luck at the next station. Destitute homeless strung-out junkies shuffled around me, illustrating the large corpus of texts about the person, he or she, who chooses to descend into hell while preventing the spirits of the dead from coming near the blood.

You kept going, recoiling from shades who really were helpless, each one with his story, his lament, his rhythm and long-playing record—Agamemnon, Alcinous, Antiope—the main thing is not to let them near the sacrificial blood, the main thing is to sustain your indifference to their, so to speak, situation, to leave them behind in the translucent dusk with their needles, their babies, their shopping carts lifted from the grocery chain Omnia Mea. The main thing is not to think too much, not to make all those heartbreaking speculations about why they're sitting there slumped over, pushing needles into their black veins. Once, in a fit of anthropological passion, I let myself look too long at some-one, and he ran after me and hit me—gently, feebly, playfully.

I lived in that city for eight years—in my time (now it seems this time of mine was when everything happened in the present, not burdened by past or future). I know that city well. I know the places that are peaceful, or scary, or empty, or wonderful. Its topography is my anatomy, meaning, it's also my biography, something like that.

Approaching these ratpiss@squeal (enough, you'll get your hand slapped) memories, I turned south on Market Street into a seedy, pitiful, filthy realm. Though, really, who is clean, doesn't every body stink and ache and agonize and hunger and sense danger. South of Market Street the same shops as before selling the ever-popular fake torturewear made a big show of it: What's your heart's desire? Whips—garrotes—Spanish boots?

That earlier time (my time) my companion had a heart's desire. He had loved a thousand times, visited a thousand rooms, seen a thousand things. And now he was luring me in.

I remember it was the bra with iron nails pointing inward that undid me. Fuck, I thought, what is this, why does tender me have to witness this and try it on? How does it look? Does it make me look good?

My companion liked the price and didn't bargain almost, he also found the fit satisfactory: suitably unbearable. Later there was a lot of blood from the nails.

I-she (during the procedure I-she preferred to think of herself in the third person, thus doing what she could to cover the drawn flesh of the first person)—this I has so many clever tactics. The writer Babel's widow, an attractive iron lady subway builder, ideally lacking a sense of humor, tells us with surprise: "When I asked him why he writes stories with a nonfictional narrator, Babel said, 'That way the stories can be shorter, since I don't have to describe who the narrator is, what he's wearing, where he's been . . .'"

She-I, by now not dressed in anything (Medea's daughter, who tore off her skin along with the poisoned underwear), stood in the shower and blood ran across her toes, thanks to which they started looking like tender new white-pink radishes.

In a tense lazy voice my companion was calling to me from the bedroom—Are you ready?

Oh world of fantasies (now you're walking along Moscow Prospect, a children's paradise where worlds reveal themselves: Washer World, Refrigerator World, Plumbing World)—a taxonomy of games! 148. He uses the whip only on the face; he likes red faces. 149. He whips all parts of the body indiscriminately: He spares nothing, including the face, vagina, breasts. 150. He uses a bullwhip to land two hundred strokes along the backs of young men ages sixteen to twenty.

The blood, the sperm, the shit washed off, the instruments frayed, the makeup ran (black-and-silver shadows, sparkles mixed into the asphalt).

Torture—what can we say about it? What is the plot? The main event? Who is the hero?

In the moment you're enduring torture, digging your nails into the skin of your palms—what are you waiting for, what expecting? What are you remembering? Do you remember yourself?

South of Market Street they offer whatever you want at a negotiated price, instruments of sweet torture, domination, and submission—and this time I'm struck by the fact that people with crude imaginations need implements, costumes, scenery for the whole thing. Whereas people with delicate, inflamed imaginations find physical enactment laughable and unnecessary, undesirable. Beside the point.

Cosplay torture, how can it compare to real destruction, intangible, bodiless, relentless, knowing neither beginning nor end but going on forever, penetrating everything, tracking you down wherever you are—even, can you believe it, even here.

And that is why I am wandering around San Francisco right now. What, you ask, is my itinerary, my mission, my rationale? Perhaps it's this: Two weeks ago I received a letter from the very man who consigned me to fiery Gehenna at the tender age when. What age shall we consider tender? When the condition of the spiritual muscles is such that everything in you succumbs, submits to molding, to outside pressure, while you are still pure clay—firm soft damp you sit you stand you fall you disappear at the command of your pedagogue; then humiliation and disappointment consign you to the fire a second time—at a different temperature range—and you become very solid and very breakable. But at fifteen—hey, come on in, take whatever you want.

In order to do this, to send you on a journey to hell, the author of the letter from the underworld did not, I assure you, require whips, spikes, or any other subtle menacing accoutrements. The author of the recently arrived letter took advantage, back then, of the pliancy, the thirst, the pathetic hunger, everything an adolescent's being emits like a dying skunk—in unbelievable shameful quantities. Reeking sprays of eager attention.

There was the classic age difference of thirty-five long years (the late-night call—my heart, it hurts so much, it's bulging and shrinking—don't let me die alone). Modeling his behavior on his philosophy, he always approached from a distance, always with a teasing formality.

What are you doing now, my lady? Are you dressed?

You lay in the dark in your grandmother's orange flannel nightshirt XXL (a gift straight from a failing heart—I could use it like a tent and fit my whole suddenly swelling and maturing child's body into it) and couldn't stop thinking about what was happening on the other side of the city, his heart was bulging and shrinking, it might shudder and leap out of his body, it might explode like a supernova and become stardust. Besides conversations about the highly explosive heart, you can be sure that other organs and procedures were discussed, but there's the rub, as the Danish prince said— then, as now, having tested all the instruments and devices and blunted many of them, you know that everything is negotiable, and only one thing has no price for that refined icy white-hot voice coming through the receiver of the yearning adolescent's phone, the voice that commands: I am dying—you must appear before me like a leaf before the grass, rise, Lazarus, hasten to me and be mine.

The letter I received said its author had arrived in the state of California with the purpose—you guessed it—of definitively dying, can you believe it, what a coincidence ... for him to turn up in a California paradise—and why shouldn't we, after all, have a chat about this and that before he hits the road?

Completely stunned at being ambushed by the reincarnated and yet again dying snake, I was wandering around San Francisco's worst areas in the autumn night, trying to connect different eras and manifestations of pain: Joysuffering is all the same, bleated the insatiable aesthete from across the city in his magical goat-tones.

Vice and virtue also are proximate, another aesthete droned—if you told the Herzog that people nonetheless have notions of justice and injustice, he would answer that these ideas are relative. I am not going to restrain my impulses just to please God. Nature endowed me with them, and if I were to resist them, I would be going against my Natural self. I am just an instrument in Nature's hands. Thus modeling his behavior on his philosophy, from his youth the Herzog launched upon the most shameful and vivid adventures. After perpetrating a crime he would enter a state of total indifference toward his victim and what had just taken place.

Toward what had just not taken place. Because, honestly, what did take place, the bewildered reader asks. After spending the whole night wrapped in visions, like freezing bed warmers, of his death, the adolescent girl would race to catch the first subway train, run into his room—he would lift his scaly dragon eyelids and spit out with disgust: Why did you come—you're pathetic. Get out of here.

This was repeated many, many times.

Trying to figure out (a) do I go relish the sight of my soul's destroyer in the agonies of chemo; (b) what the hell kind of plot was it that led me here to the glittering asphalt to put yet another moral challenge to myself—will I again enter the den of the expiring dragon who once devoured, feasted upon, your heart (like this: yum-yum-yum). Probably that very question is the main event, the plot—without which a respectable unsuccessful life, or a respectable prose, cannot live, cannot hold together. A good question always needs to be asked twice. Once again I visited: the pain event.

Hasten to me and be mine. I have to tell you, I'm completely unattractive now. His face with its refined features and rather beautiful eyes but repellent mouth and teeth, his white body with nothing growing on it, his small but shapely ass, later on we'll talk about his other predilections. Tiresias, what have I become, what am I doing, how did I get here, what am I writing and with what?

Tiresias exhaled carefully: "I think this is prose. This text doesn't break into phrases or even fragments. Something binds it very tightly. I also very much like—and this is incredibly difficult and rarely achieved—how the words seem like they're fused with one another. I can't express it more precisely but that's how it feels to me, and when you're successful (several times), I'm envious, that is, I regret failing at it so often. So much for aesthetics. As far as ethics and psychology—I have nothing to say." Tiresias, after all, was a stylist. He taught you how to injure readers with iron words, how to delight them, how to make them become themselves—while keeping the voice firm and gentle. Then they will look at you like you're the burning bush: you'll see.

What would he do with your heart this time? Take it to replace his own disintegrating one? Once again spew it from his mouth? The mechanism of the summons was key, like the salty trickle a vampire needs to sustain his delicate-brawny life. It would mean a return to the question, a return to my twenty-year-old self, a return to the scene—turn right and you'll see the corner store, behind it the dumpster, the garden. They mark an itinerary of pain as you run knowing to comfort and possess him, but he's always disgusted with you, displeased.

Now you're again being enticed by Tristan's enticement, your heart is like an oyster being shucked with a short knife. (What does the heart have to do with it, he once said, it's well known that the soul is found in the throat. Everything he said you clutched in your hand and carried into the world of mediocrity, you kept it close, held it to your ear like a seashell and smiled like an idiot. He taught you, he instilled in you: There is no difference between good and evil, there is only the fear of desire, fear of insensibility-boredom, and fear of death, they're all the same thing—you must fight these manifestations of fear. Everything is a question of style.)

54. He wants the girl to go to confession and waits for the moment she emerges to fuck her in the mouth. 55. He engages a prostitute for a Mass conducted in his own chapel and comes as the benediction ends.

Afterward, feeling sated and burdened by indifference toward his victim, who radiated the teeeedious stench of longing, desire, empathy, he told everyone who was ready to listen, the whole chattering city, that his so-called victim was herself responsible (since there is no difference between just and unjust) for everything (for what?) and therefore cannot be regarded as a victim but from this day forward must be considered a rapacious climber who sank her sharp claws into the failing, brittle Pierrot like a vicious shrew, an ugly smelly little beast. She must be swept into the drain with a mop.

And now that I am climbing out of the drain (in a real sense, my whole life has gone into this process of extracting myself from the drain), I'm supposed to go to him, lying there saturated with the ennobling juices of chemotherapy, and say, I remember no evil, I remember nothing.

God help you—but I remember everything. I cannot. Forget.

How shall we conclude this story?

On one of those mornings when, tormented by his midnight shamanism, I ran to him—to my totsky/myshkin, my frigid nastasia—he sat turned to the window, his face, as always, filled with *almost* visible sickly boredom, as though the whole world were filled with boredom like a stench. And suddenly something like pity came over him, ran through his body: he bowed and placed his palms over your palms— but then he recoiled and breathed his refrain: Get out of here.

I carried this inside me for almost twenty years—through all the beddings and cries of pleasure, I carried it in bras with nails pointing in and out, and in silk corsets that left pink traces on my fleshy back, sewn with beads which I so passionately learned to cast before swine: And now you summon me, the question arises again, and, who knows, it's possible that twenty years is the term of this monstrous pregnancy and now an answer will be born. Tiresias will explain to me the meaning of this life, barely distinguishable from death, filled with shades and their impossible desires.

Just imagine it. I'd walk into the terrifying hospital room (cut the melodrama, why terrifying—this is Stanford, after all), I'd walk into the resplendent hospital room, and you'd be lying there, full of your own internal poison and now an external one, occupied with their mixing and combining within yourself. I'd lean over you, over You ("never use the familiar with someone you love")—and something would come over me. Like one of countless Justines or Eugenies, I spent those years hoping to gain your approval: I did not profess virtue but sowed your lessons like dragons' teeth. With tubes sticking out of all your orifices, my teacher, my dear Franval, take me at last into your affirming embrace and we will be at peace. Maybe we'd pathetically caress each other again, or maybe we'd die instantly, like the homeless during an early freeze, and they'd collect our bodies in the morning.

# HAIR STICKS

*To Alexandra Miya*

"PIN ME," I said, "pin my hair, please, so it's like yours, I want to go in the water." Silently, with her usual attentiveness, she took the hair sticks out of her hair and skillfully used them to fix a bun on the back of my head. She didn't find it all that hard—our Ashkenazi hair was made of the same stuff, tangly, heavy, prickly as felt. Only the color was a little different: Hers was bronze, almost the color of beets, almost like the manganese stains in a sink—like when the sun is almost in its burrow, its billiard pocket. My hair, though, is like grass in October under a feeble sun—brown like fur, frizzy. Or like the destroyed, desiccated seaweed the surf rhythmically spits out onto the sand. She colored her gray, but I was incredibly proud of my few dead strands—like a self-promoter shoving invitations to an *exclusive* party in the faces of yawning guests.

I loved how easily she twisted my hair into a bun, and as I sat in the water, I kept reaching up to touch it as if it were a helmet, imagining myself as the gloomiest and least flighty of goddesses, the upstart know-it-all Pallada, whom Apollo and Aphrodite made fun of as they groped each other with abandon in the sunlit back of the classroom.

When I crawled onto dry land like an ancient creature, she looked at me over her sunburned shoulder and said with sullen conviction: "Hair sticks are essential." They must be hard, they must be sharp, and they must not bend—"like these ones, you can have them."

Getting ready for bed I regretfully freed my hair and put the hair sticks inside the book I was carrying around like a self-important burgher—a Bible with crumpled, disintegrating, greasy corners—I knew this book practically by heart, actually no, I knew it completely by heart—and why was I reading it over and over again?

As always when you reread a book, you do it not for the sake of understanding but for the pure physical joy of touching the same letters with your lips, recognizing familiar faces by feel. Here's Marina Malich sitting outside her locked apartment—inside, her husband, Danny, is having sex, he left a note on the door asking her to wait before coming in, he was considerate, he was thinking about her—he could be in there with her friend, or her sister Olga. Here's Marina Malich making her way out of the dead city, where even the executioners don't have it so good—you're losing teeth and your hair is falling out, it's time to go; the best hope of Leningraders, the ones who could still move and feel fear, were the Germans—they'll put you in a cowshed, in the cow shit, feed you on silage, they'll beat you, but they'll kindly pull you from the noose just in time whenever you attempt suicide. Here's Marina Malich on the inhabited desert island of freedom, in Paris, seducing her mother's husband, a balding, mild, affectionate shameless person. Her mother, who had left the girl behind several revolutions and wars ago, somewhat stung by her daughter's adroitness, puts on her lipstick, arranges the netting on her hat, and with firm steps (though her ankles aren't what they used to be, they're thicker now) walks to the Soviet consulate to ask them to send her daughter back—if possible, to a Siberian labor camp. La Sibérie.

Everything about her life seemed to me significant and familiar and tangible—I would imagine Marina Malich in the rich variety of her circumstances, I rotated her life like the tube of a kaleidoscope—the pattern would change but stay the same: her proud asymmetrical face frozen in surprise at how her life kept shrinking but still death didn't come. After reciting to myself a carefully chosen sinister bit from Marina Malich's adventures, I would fall asleep—a hair stick poked out from Glotser's book like a plot-generating spindle: black and unbending.

My friend would peek into my room and turn off the light. I always leave the light on in all the rooms of houses where I happen to spend the night—it's better to meet darkness in the light, with the light on.

Later on they all suddenly had little girls cranking up inside them, and I began thinking about them constantly—my redheaded friend had one, and my friend with the light brown hair and eyes like shards of malachite, and the one with hair like cheerful straw (all the life's inside, so the wild strawberries dried up), who wanted her daughter so much that she yelled it on the squares of Petersburg, "Would you just get here, my love?" I could understand that impatience—when my daughter started living inside me, I went to Nonna and said, "It will be a girl." She raised her white-blond eyebrows in confusion and said, "Naturally, who else would she be?" A joke in reverse.

A girl inside a girl—a pleonasm, a grotesque matryoshka, *that's going too far*, pain inside of pain, a girl swells up and tears at the seams to birth herself a self. So she can take a look, almost from the outside, at what she's already experienced, almost from the inside.

When the sun sets over the isle of the Amazons, we lie down together and begin staring, sniffing at each other. There lies my defiant, frowning daughter, a sweet pungent smell on her breath. She puts her monkey hands and legs on me, now squeezes one of my curls in her hand, fusses, then opens one eye in her sleep like the bad sister in that frightening story about Little Khavroshechka, or the feast of the vigilant Cyclops. To say she does not resemble me would be an understatement. This verdict was handed down by my forever driving instructor Walter: In a moment of despair (lesson 38), he pulled up to our house, where you could observe a bucolic scene of resurrecting the garden: An inspired Nonna and Frosya were breathing hard over their plantings. "Yeah," Walter drawled, "your mother's gorgeous, your daughter's gorgeous, who do you take after?" I didn't find his question unfair or unexpected, but I told Walter that I was now going to crash his driving-school car into a concrete post. "No, you won't," he grimly said, "I've got my foot on the brake."

All of my women friends are remarkable beauties. One of my favorite entertainments: to watch as passersby turn their heads; how, as we enter a café, there's a moment of strained silence. I learned my most bitter lesson-disaster on the subject of observing the observers while visiting a European capital flooded by brown waters, you'll remember when, where a being with a bright name and very bright hair and eyes and an endearing way of rolling her *rrrrr*'s (*aimez-vouz Benjamine Kaverrrrine?*) decided to seek shelter at my place from the harassments of the sun. She found me trying to wash some stinking socks over a stinking corroded sink. "How many do you have left?" "Eleven," I answered with the cold hatred of a sniper looking from behind his cover at the enemy. "Could you take a break? I'd like you to read— a few words I wrote to you." I read the words and found what she was looking for. She melted in my hands and on my tongue *not mediately*, she disintegrated like the Snow Maiden: I want, I really want to jump the fire, grandma, grandpa. All right, then: jump. I rolled my *rrrr* into her and gave her back her own, she opened herself up and lay there like a mangled oyster from a still life with light filtering through a goblet onto a lemon peel black with mold. Then like an incompetent murderer I fled the small ruin I'd created with my competent hands: I flew off to empty and sunny California to realize my so-called destiny—to live life not relying on anyone, nor pretending to be anyone's rock, just watching the beauties with the brimming eye of a crocodile on a diet. And really, am I, say, the sister or mother of Marina Malich—just an instrument of the power to wound, an odorous deaf Narcissus, who, reduced, paralyzed, never had a clue the nymph Echo was calling for help? "Nevermore will I touch my reflection with hand, or tongue, or what burns at the moment of parting, I will not disturb my reflection"—that was my vow.

And now in California spring bellies are bursting, and inside them new girls are swaying. They feel cramped, hot, peaceful: They're preparing for transformations. Little red bilberries of clay—they will be kneaded and caressed and evaluated and assessed by those who have their foot on the brake. They will be splayed, squeezed, suffocated, filled with cries, and when they no longer have the strength to endure it, they will resort to their own. They will seek connection, and power, and freedom. "So then," Dinka impatiently pronounced, her voice once again changed its timbre, moving from a self-protective kittenish whimper to calm and commanding tones, "I don't know what you're thinking about, right now you just need to think about *what* we are going to drink, that's all." And she headed for the bar, angry and unbending.

# SESTRORETSK, KOMAROVO

*To Ostap*

## 1985

"IT'S ABOUT time you wrote a trip," my companion laughed, flicking his divinely long fingers. Enchanted by this movement, I had trouble focusing on his words, distracted, as always, by form at the expense of content.

My friend is Japanese, a melancholy and whimsical interpreter of Russian poetry, and handsome, so it often happened that the better part of his conversation just flew past, scattered by the agitated morning light radiating from this most *real* beauty: you want to squint, turn away.

"Ah," I said, "a trip ... oh very funny, the poet's dreaded, pointless p(r)ose."

"Not at all," my companion said, smiling, "a railroad prose, a nice little prose that stretches as far as it can. A prose that's like time, so you feel like there's too much of it, it's everywhere—so you have as much prose as you have time. Not like poetry, which exits-explodes, and then what are you supposed to do? An act—an erection—an ejaculation (irresistible monstrosities from a medical encyclopedia)—you get your half hour's entertainment and then what? You go to mother prose."

And which trip shall we choose to fill out time's uneven

landscape, as it spreads out before us after the poem's sweet contusion?

How about this one.

No, first I'll tell you about something else—not a trip but a location, something like a prison.

My papa was not well.

Sometimes his face would take on a somewhat violet, actually more of a bluish, shade; his mouth would jerk to the side and words definitively stopped coming out. This meant that, once again, it was time for us to head to a sanatorium.

That year fate decreed we would take the waters in the city of Sestroretsk on the eastern shore of the shallow (depth of 2.5 to 3.5 meters at 200 meters from the beach) Sestroretsk Bay on the Gulf of Finland in the Baltic Sea. Lining the shore is a wooded crest of dunes and hills, interrupted by riverbeds and small lakes, ponds and areas of bare rock. Sandy ("golden") beach up to 50 meters wide. Not far from the sanatorium is Lake Razliv, created by the construction of a dam on the river. According to the Soviet census of 1989, Sestroretsk had a population of 35,498. The overwhelming majority worked at the sanatorium or leaned on the beer bar at the depot huddling against the Baltic wind, or they did both in shifts.

Why Sestroretsk? Each time my papa was suffused with his violet, Mama would procure from the mysterious-generous agency Prophylactics a vacation for two and, without missing a beat, mercilessly substitute me for herself in the formula—me, a puffy adolescent brimming with gloomy life-force. No one was given a choice. Of all the prescribed procedures (the mineral baths, the terrifying mud baths that were like being buried alive, the Charcot showers, the swims in the barely heated pool past old women looking like jellyfish), the hardest to endure was Papa's silence.

Sometimes the physical strain of this exercise grew unbearable, but opportunities to take a reprieve were limited: the library with its collected works of Soviet classics (conceited virgins) and pulp fiction (used tired beckoning strumpets); the bay with its antitank barriers of ice and narrow strips of sand that was still dead, the consistency of asphalt. The scent of the hidden sea made its way up through the ice: my nostrils flared like a hunting dog's whose prey was here, right here. We stood together and watched the icy red sun fall into the icy red sea at four o'clock. At the spectacle's finale, he would always say, "It's not good to look at the sun—you'll go blind." A laconic didact, he carved his aphorisms into my heart: "Either a girl should have a good figure, or she should be cheerful—decide what you can manage" (but I can't manage any of it, I despaired). "If a girl smells like a little fox, she should take special care with her hygiene" (and truly I did smell of a wild animal unknown to him, and following that scent was no simple thing).

There were also, of course, our hikes to the dining hall, the only locus of our dialogues—seemingly animated (by comparison to everything else) discussions of the menu, which presented three delicious options every day—Papa would cautiously (due to his pain, he did everything cautiously) raise his black brows and say: So what will it be, Polina, the carrot cutlets, or the goulash, or the rice porridge?

After our repast, we would go for a walk. Back then he

rarely left me alone, feeling, I suppose, a certain responsibil-
ity—like a prison guard's—and we split between us the
sensation of the cold warming in places and rust everywhere. Pine needles, banisters, the outdoor pool not fit for
human use.

On Sundays actors would arrive at the sanatorium. They
were the most pathetic specimens in the Leningrad region's
habitat, actors whose unprofessionalism and fateful blows
had driven them far beyond the bounds of success and ambition.

On Saturdays they would hang up a poster next to the
menu: "The best actors in the world, either for tragedy, com-
edy, history, pastoral, pastoral-comical, historical-pastoral,
tragical-historical, tragical-comical-historical-pastoral, scene
individable, or poem unlimited. Seneca cannot be too heavy,
nor Plautus too light. For the law of writ and the liberty,
these are the only men."

A flabby, distracted woman with hair dyed a carrot color
and a Crimplene dress shining with sequins, would breathe
out, between gasps for air, excerpts from, say, Berggolts or
Panova, while the victims of ulcerative colitis and gastritis
sighed and fidgeted from embarrassment and boredom.
Aroused by my encounter with the Beautiful, I went back
to my small room. Papa lay there turned to the wall, moaning with pain in a regular, tedious rhythm.

An ulcer of the duodenum was eating him from inside,
like that smelly Spartan fox cub; all those years I imagined
it as a terrible, vicious little god, a ruthless cunning beast
with twelve fingers.

I would cover my head with my pillow and repeat *random*
words that meaninglessly echoed and mirrored each other.

## 1991 (A YEAR BEFORE HIS DEATH)

This time the magician-prophylactery transported us to that pine-dune realm the reading public associates with the slow, winter evening walks of a heavyset woman with a thick voice, sounding as though someone had placed an iron bell over your head or a cassette tape was getting stuck and slowing down (*"Professor Barskova, what's going on, is this a man or a woman speaking?"*). It's a woman speaking.

By then I was fifteen years old—the age of premeditated protest. My premeditated protest took the form of defending myself against my father's silence by reading successive volumes of Dumas père on a swing set near the sanatorium's trails. Dumas was not an accidental choice—there were fifty volumes in his (frustratingly incomplete) collected works. Swinging along with me were Milady with her bleeding shoulder and lopped-off head, the extravagant harebrain of the Siberian snows, Pauline Gueble, and, fussing over a bundle containing the head of her lover, the hot-to-trot Marguerite de Navarre—they seemed like convincing models to emulate, covered as I was in the shame of the marks of sexual overripening.

But the most beloved, the most familiar of all was *The Count of Monte Cristo*. At this point Papa announced that he had to go into the city on business and was leaving me on my own for a day. Thus it happened that I decided to follow my Count to freedom—to escape imprisonment in the terrifying canvas sack, that is, to set out immediately for the Komarovo cemetery. Why so morbid, the annoyed reader asks?

*Ruinlust*? A desire to visit the shades of the great? Something along those lines. What I'd decided was to find a new father for myself, a *better* father. At least the shade of a new father.

There was no mysticism involved—only pragmatism. (When it comes down to it, the person telling you these stories is someone who decided, after the death of her beloved, to get baptized from purely bureaucratic considerations: Say that Judgment Day arrives, I reasoned, and the gloomy, broad-shouldered gatekeeper doesn't let me see him, doesn't let me tell him that I found the strength to live and love after everything you messed up, my dear—just because I don't have a little cross? Not a chance! But that's another story.)

In this story (the camera swings around and freezes), I despondently pick through the gloomy volumes of the Library of World Literature on my parents' dusty bookshelves, behind them appears a mixed forest of this and that, and there I uncover, inside a thin volume of translations of a legendary Chinese poet-alcoholic, two curious emblems: an inscription of a too-private, sentimental nature and a photograph of the translator. The conjuncture of these fateful signs left me with no doubt: The unknown passionate sinologist could thereby immediately be crowned the awaited father.

How could there be any doubt? I went to the mirror and did a quick check—everything lined up: the high forehead, the aristocratic chiseled nose, the subtle mocking mouth, the cool mocking eyes. I swelled with pride from recognition and expectation, like Pippi Longstocking: So that's where she got her superhuman strength. Now I know! That's where I get my reserve, my weighty presence, my chilly manner and air of fortune's favorite.

This wad of tepid imaginings lived and throbbed inside me from then on, and when my papa's silence reached an arctic temperature, I would look at him with a smile and think: That's okay, you know, that other father, he wouldn't refuse to talk, we would read *The Count of Monte Cristo* aloud to each other . . . that sort of thing.

So I viewed the departure of the silent one as fate's command, make your way, it spake, to the Komarovo cemetery, there (she had done her pathetic research as a foundling of Leningrad literature), there next to the grave of his remarkable mother (maybe I also have a grandmother—I mean, had one?—"a face with a vague expression her chin slightly jutting out her hair is regrettable she dyes it red giving her an autumnal and at the same time artificial look she loves to play preference so much she almost gave herself a second heart attack but then a miracle occurs—she starts writing again—and accomplishes wonders")—there he, too, rests.

The walk from the sanatorium to the cemetery took about two hours *at a vigorous pace*. Her pace was never vigorous. Her path went past the train station, then along the lake, she crossed the railroad tracks and almost fell, there was a strong smell of tar and machine oil. From the train station to the cemetery reached a gradually diminishing stream of gawkers and legitimate grieving relatives.

How eagerly she walked from slab to cross, from merit star to cobblestone. Beneath the markers reposed Soviet and anti-Soviet celebrities, whose doctors had prescribed the invigorating Baltic breezes and fine beach sand that stings your eyes.

Now at last—here he is. Right next to his mama. The frondeur and slacker next to the stubborn worker bee who sometimes managed to buzzzzz out prose of absolutely tragic purity. Together this famous mother-and-son could be considered an ideal pietà, an allegory of Leningrad writing: not fully expressed, not fully educated, eaten from within by compromise and, in the end—irresistible. I had saved for the road leftovers from the sanatorium breakfast—a cheese pastry and an apple. I sat on the ground next to his grave, in the full sun. I laid out our Soviet high tea. I felt like he'd come, he'd joined me. Like they'd been waiting for you, they wouldn't sit down to eat without you, they were checking the clock and looking out the window.

And what, really, was I going to do with these new acquaintances, this newly acquired father? I wasn't much thinking about it at the time. Just as in the moment you conceive a new passion, you don't think about the obstacles, the routine, the pathetic farewells, or any impossibility at all but float in rays of certainty and the foretaste of intimacy: What will it be like this time? Which part of your body will your friend's hands, lips, life touch first? I simply enjoyed the newfound sappy feeling that I was no longer alone in the world, that the beautiful mother and son sleeping behind the railing, if only the magical power of my pastry crumbs could wake them, would take pity on me and maybe even, after sniffing my scent, accept me as their own.

## DENOUEMENT

Need I say, since you've already guessed it, dear reader, that the well-built Komarovo wit had no direct relevance to me, and hence none to you. More like indirect relevance. That stroll out of town didn't solve anything.

Birch syrup in a huge cloudy jar—Papa always brought me one on his birthday, May the 5th, in a mesh bag, that's how spring would begin.

What was it that was so cloudy—the syrup or the glass? Impossible to say.

After he died I found in his drawer a large packet of my poems copied out in a perfect, fastidious hand—when he was alive not a word about them passed between us.

As a final sign of this life, a cockroach crawled out of his pipe and went on its way.

# DONA FLOR AND HER GRANDMOTHER

FORTY years ago an aged Anaïs Nin attended the inaugural ceremony of the college where fate has cast me ashore. The procedure took place in an empty field: The diminutive Anaïs walked into that empty field and threw open her cape, and the assembled brotherhood of great minds and celebrities saw her famous dark little soon-to-be-deceased body.

It was the month of May, and the wind lightly caressed her tiny form.

Anaïsanaïs, it was thanks to your diaries that I felt the jealous ambition (why can she do this, and not me?) to talk about what you're not supposed to talk about—because what else are you going to talk about?

It was a bizarre summer.

You died, and then they held a service for you in Preobrazhensky Cathedral, and I stood at your open coffin and cried and wondered how this must look to the casual observer. My tears brought relief but they also washed away any possible thread of connection to the living: a sinkhole was forming, a mudslide, that was taking me under, deeper and deeper with each theatrical, well-tempered sob.

I was, however, determined not to go under and to give definite form to what had happened. Every evening at the appointed hour I would ride the subway to Nevsky Prospect, to where the Duma's red tower is, and commence standing-smoking across the way from a certain spot.

I was convinced that the iron regularity of this vigil would, if not cancel, then somehow change the fact that you had set out alone to cross the road and either turned back or tripped, and I would never be able to grasp the impact, the pain, the surprise with which your consciousness ended. Yours was the frivolous, busy consciousness of an enthusiastic literary juggler, one that didn't embrace anything or anyone very deeply or for the long run but that, for the short run, gave itself completely to the new object of fascination. Which it would then betray. But suddenly, in an awkward casting change, I ended up playing the betrayer, since you had left the stage. By the sympathetic light of the slowly fading white nights, I studied the pothole in the asphalt, the boots of people walking by, the half-erased lines of the cross-walk, hoping to find a way to soothe this thing like something had slammed me from the left and winded me. Across the way on Nevsky a sign glowed—the name of a store with a tic in one blinking letter, and thus I amused myself for three or so hours every evening.

When it got dark, I would go home, jiggle the bent key in the bent lock, lie down with my face to the couch's dingy fabric. Neither Mama nor the cat could make themselves come into my room. They were having an argument crisis.

After a month of my standing guard, my mother had the inspired thought that something *must be done*—meaning that a watch was to be set for the watchman.

It was decided I should be placed into my babushka's care—in Siberia.

My babushka, who resembled a kombucha mushroom, lived in a certain Siberian city in anxious weblike union with her two daughters and their families.

Mama reasoned that this guard unit would be sufficient to ensure I didn't do anything to myself. She couldn't have known that, at the time, I was completely incapable of performing any action whatsoever. All the life went out and away from me (me, in whom so much life was invested!), and, except for that pedestrian crossing on Nevsky Prospect, it made absolutely no difference to me where I was or where I went (and just yesterday my sense of place and of direction were my most developed senses!).

The next islet of memory to swim up (I imagine memory works like a soup into which you dip your spoon like an oar, and surprising things rise to the surface in a surprising sequence). My aunt, a manic eternal beauty with sapphire eyes (that's what Bunin would have called them, sitting out the long dreary night with Chekhov hacking, trying out words; Knipper scrutinizes her flawless little brow in the mirror, smiles, and exits)—yes, sapphire eyes on a dark tanned face that always smelled of honey and wormwood—took me to the forest and to the water. My aunt taught me many things: how to recognize a kingfisher, how to gather stone brambleberries then mash them through cheesecloth and pour the blood over whipped cream in the morning. At that point nothing had yet happened in the world, and your cat Liuska still slept on your pillow with a frog's leg sticking out of her mouth.

My aunt taught me to race across the hills on a sinister chase after a fleeing family of white mushrooms, or advance through pine glades, cutting down villages of butter mushrooms— "You squeeze it right there, like that."

It was from her that you inherited the rush and predatory joy you feel when you breathe in the smell of the Siberian forests, and all of it is yours and you yourself are all of it, you belong to it and serve it. The childish name Lyolya suited her and seemed like a greeting from a certain devotee of words and sounds who also lay in the dark in his narrow bed remembering mushrooms, and moss, and harsh wet grass.

Lying in the dark in my narrow bed, I could hear my aunt talking to her husband behind the wall:

"Who is going to marry her? She'll never get married if she keeps on like this... She can't do anything! She knows nothing about you-know-what—what it means to have a family."

To avoid interrupting their conversation with my wet sobbing, I got up and went to the water—to the Obsk Sea. I sat on the pier and listened to the bream swimming—they were sick with intestinal worms and didn't have the strength to get to the bottom. Here I am, I thought, just like the infected fish, cast out from life's sludge and murk onto a meaningless surface.

On the weekends they would take me into the city to visit Babushka.

My babushka baked very small and very buttery cabbage pierogi, which her whole family would eat with appreciative moans. Then we would proceed to the official portion of our visit. It (the official portion) was I.

"By the way," Lyolya said, "we decided not to tell her that he, you know, died, she does have high blood pressure."

"So what did you tell her?"

"You know, that he dumped you and you're really upset about it."

On the weekends Babushka would instruct me in the art of love, meaning, she would explain how to make you come back and love me *forever*, right then and there. Our lessons were conducted in the obligatory presence of a member of the household—if not Lyolya, then one of her offspring, jokesters with lynx eyes, or her older sister, the completely opposite and acutely depressed Bella. The whole household was on the alert lest I show any sign of weakening, but it was pointless to suspect me of anything. My conversations with Babushka about the secrets of ruling the feckless male heart were more calming, more soothing, than when my cousin Anton sat with me afterward and stroked my hair, so sorry and embarrassed about my misfortune.

Not to mention, Babushka clearly knew what she was talking about: When a well-endowed, widowed medico arrived in her dead postwar mining town in the Kuzbass, it was she—with ten years on him and a trying character, owner of four starving children of various colors and markings—

who claimed him for the entirety of his long, happy life. Babushka took Igor Mikhailovich's death very hard and fell into a pitiful helpless state until I showed up with my glaring deficits in the area of domestic happiness, which needed to be made up. For many Sundays Babushka showed me how to cook, do the laundry, clean the house, dress properly, choose perfumes, do my hair, all so that you, God forbid, wouldn't leave me.

Perfumes should be just a little bit acrid, the filling for cabbage pierogi should be delicate, your husband must have no hint that your period has come—a detail of blissful marital life that struck me, somehow fusing with my aunt's horrifying refrain, "Don't ever show your butt / a husband is a mutt." My aunt, her mother's daughter, clearly had absorbed the essential teachings.

Then we would leave again for the forest and the water, and I would wander around, no longer a nine-year-old smeared with stone brambleberries and black mushroom slime but a huge, unrecognizable nineteen-year-old hapless bird or fish— I would lie on the moss or sit on a rock and close my eyes and think about you.

As someone possessed of a not superficially constituted, capricious yet strong will, I kept trying to turn 2-D into 3-D, to see you for just one second walking toward me with your headphones on (for some reason, you were always listening to the Beatles) down that same accursed Nevsky—it all began and ended there. So I am here to tell you: It can't be done, in the sense that I wasn't able to do it.

You didn't exist anywhere anymore, and no matter how

extraordinarily hard I tried to picture your face and your mouth twisting at the culmination of the act as I stroked myself with a nimble, consoling hand, no matter how I tried to resurrect, tone by tone, your mewing—I came up with nothing. I was still alone.

A degree of strain and uncertainty—from the trips to town, from the raised hopes ("Oh, after the lingonberry tart, no one can resist you!") to the empty waters and back—made itself felt. I fell ill with a strange disease which my cousin-doctor diagnosed as "maybe cholera." Lyolya turned as sapphire as her eyes, braced her arms against the wall, and said, *"What am I going to tell Nonna?"* At which point the eldest sister, the sad Bella, said to no one in particular, "We will give her bloodsip."

Bloodsip is one of those magical herbs (remember Gauf, Little Longnose, the wise goose?) in which you place your hopes when there is no hope left. The name matches the intensity of its effect; I'll spare you the details, I'm no Marquis de Sade. We went to the village market to get it—I was nauseous, disoriented, dizzy. Lyolya, afraid to leave me home alone, held me firmly by the hand. It was a very bright and sunny day, Joe Dassin was floating above the market confirming that if you ever disappeared, that would be the absolute end. And how! The market bustled and bubbled, and toothy pig heads swam in vats—they swam and smiled as part of my fascinating dream. Lyolya bought peaches and bit into them with her tiny, sugar-white cat teeth: You must be strong, my dear, she said, giving me a smile.

But I forgot to tell you the main thing, which is that she is an artist, and in our windbreakers we would gather the scratchy, sour- and bitter-smelling, frightening Siberian flowers, and she would draw them—always resembling her, a little tousled, the shadows falling slightly off the mark, much too colorful. It turned out she was right: I never did get married because I can't do anything except be delighted and horrified at the senseless beauty of things (the evening, the wind, the tired Caravaggian face of the man quietly sleeping next to me).

# REAPER OF LEAVES

*To Mark Lipovetsky, with gratitude for
lessons in loving Soviet literature*

## WHERE WILL THE STARLINGS MAKE THEIR NESTS, THE ONES WITHOUT A NESTING BOX?

I want to see all the way through him, as though he were a frozen January frog or a newborn eel, and reacquaint us with him, though we'll hardly welcome the renewed acquaintance. I mean to peer inside that machinery of word production, the machinery which goes by the name Bianki, and glimpse what has never been seen before. Influenced, perhaps, by his belief that hidden, invisible life is always more enthralling, more impressive, more elaborate than what submits to the indifferent eye hastening toward a conclusion, I find it comforting to think that nature is not what we imagine—nature not in the lofty sense of the great and lofty poet but in the plain sense of the poet who never developed, the awkward poet.

It turns out that while we're floundering in snow and finding ice everywhere, underneath, deep under, spring not only has quickened but is gathering-growing in earnest. Down in the burrows, in darkness and stench, newborns of the next harvest are crawling, water is pooling, dead plants are ready to come alive, and roots spread to clutch at a new spring.

But where do we look for him, this observer of nature? And how will we recognize him when we meet him? The man who is my subject today did everything he could to cover his tracks, to draw predators and hunters away from his lair—both those who surrounded him back then and those who came later. The first predators and hunters were the kind who by means of flattery, cajoling, torture, and forceful personal example pressured and seduced suppliers of words to assimilate, to change their nature for the sake of the things of this world—publishing and publicity, material comfort and a peaceful corner. Although the corners these lower-echelon wordsmiths got were fairly dank, the ceiling dripping into a saucer, drops splashing onto the cat's nose—he fastidiously shaking them off his whiskers, twitching his ears.

Whereas today's predators and hunters—from afar—are we, his readers, vigilant dividers of the wheat from the chaff (the hawk's pursuit, from up high) trying to consign to oblivion, to thoroughly douse in Lethe's sterile, uncreative solution, to judge and separate out the second-rate, the third-rate, the writers hopelessly trying to light a fire under the word. But the task of those writers was simply to stay alive and, if they succeeded, to preserve some small part of their real selves. Whatever that mirage meant to them—"realness"—this real part was hidden in a desk drawer, pickled in alcohol, or—and this was the most effective approach—openly displayed at the hunting grounds to deflect the interest of hounds and predators by its very availability, as though this real part were "carrion":

One of our forest correspondents reports from the Tver region: 'Yesterday while digging he turned up, along with the dirt, some kind of small beast. Its front paws have claws, on its back are some kind of knobs instead of wings, its body is covered with dark-yellow hairs like thick, short fur. It looks like both a wasp and a mole—insect or beast, what is it?' The editorial view: It is a remarkable insect that looks like a beast called a mole cricket. Whoever wants to find a mole cricket should pour water on the ground and cover the area with pieces of bark. At night mole crickets will seek out the damp spot, the dirt under the bark. That's where we'll find him.

Let's take a peek at the dirt under the bark—and see what there is to see.

## DUELING STORYTELLERS

Vitaly Valentinovich Bianki lived for work and drink, and toward the end of his life his voice reached its zenith, became almost a squeak, a mosquito falsetto, while he himself grew heavy and legless, but still he could not stop himself and kept tapping out his tracks on the typewriter with one finger. Contemporaries recall his Bunyanesque strength along with Bunyanesque slowness, the fading aristocratic charm of his gradually swelling face, looking like he'd been attacked by midges. Of these contemporaries, the one most inclined to observation wrote, "Bianki grabbed me by the legs, turned me upside down, and held me like that, laughing, not letting me go. Such an insult! It took me a long time to get over it.

I wasn't physically weak but this I couldn't handle. Humiliating! The worst thing was his strength seemed rough and way beyond mine. A useless feeling that wasn't quite envy and wasn't quite jealousy consumed me. Eventually it passed. Bianki was simple and decent. But the devil had done his work..."

But the devil had done his work.

The ethnographer of belles lettres repeats the phrase several times; it seems she likes it, it helps her diagnose the decline of her subject—a strong and benign creature warped by his own interpretation of affairs. Enter Evgeny Lvovich Shvarts, a dwarflike man with a head the shape of an egg, hands shaking from Parkinson's (sometimes he would leave the telegraph office with nothing accomplished, his hands shook so much that tracing a caterpillar of letters with the capricious rusty nib turned out to be impossible, with the line of people behind him simmering, irritable-resentful). A dwarf who utterly lacked the gift of forgiving and forgetting, of looking the other way, probably the most perceptive and fastidious member of a generation covered in spiritual sores. (And that's a sanitary way of putting it. When I try to imagine that generation's spiritual condition taking visible-palpable form—oh, what it would look like!...) Shvarts was venomous (from a monstrous capacity to feel wounded) and recklessly brave—he was one of those rare "valued persons" who refused in the fall of 1941 to be airlifted from Dystrophy City (the name is one of Bianki's later witticisms). By wintertime, they had to drag him out of there, psychotic, demented from hunger.

Photographs of him, and especially photographs of him in the company of women, stand out sharply in the general current of the time—the angular, mocking, delicate faces glow like seashells lit from within. Evgeny Shvarts was painfully large-spirited: In the "inventory" of his notebooks, he does not name the friends who made denunciations, scandalmongered, went into hysterics, blackened reputations. When you look at the minutes of official meetings where his friends acted the fool, attacking him as a talentless saboteur, and compare them to Shvarts's memoirs about these same people, you stop short in amazement—did he actually forgive them? Or did he cut off all feeling for them?

Like all the jokesters who in those golden years made careers rhyming, crowing, meowing, and bleating for *The Siskin* and *The Hedgehog*, Shvarts was a libertine; he took his own and his companions' sins allegorically. Hence his choice of genre—after all, we're talking about fairy tales and fabulists. Hence also the refrain: The devil had done his work. Shvarts was interested—and following him, so are we—in the allegory of the human soul's duel with the devil of the times, the pitiful stratagems used by those who inhabited those times as they tried both to placate and to hide from the devil.

Bianki, soon after his second stroke, said to Shvarts, "If you want to know what it's like when it hits you, just put on those glasses." On the table was a pair of black glasses, the lenses made the world look dim. Black light enveloped the storyteller Bianki toward the end. Storyteller Shvarts witnessed and grimly confirmed this.

## HOW TO TRANSLATE WHITE

Bianki's grandfather, an opera singer, had the last name
Weiss. This gentleman, at his impresario's request, translated
himself from German into Italian to go on tour in Italy—the
sound, the tune changed but the color remained. The sound
was now weightless, lofting upward like a bubble—a bubble
floating over a white, white field with just the tracks of small,
tired paws along the edge: Take a guess, children, who can
it be?

A young boy, darting up and down, passes dioramas of
mounted animals—under the silver hoof of an agitated,
dead-eyed deer with flared nostrils (if they really shoot it up,
does it make the taxidermist's job harder?) sprouts a dead
mushroom. For some reason these little glass mushrooms
are pinned all around the animals' legs—so we won't have
any doubts, just recognize these forms of nonlife with a
guilty tenderness. Above the deer's head they nailed a wood-
pecker stuffed with shavings. Observe how the bird's eye
knows no fear—it is open to the world and keenly focused.

The mounted animals were hideous, the aging Bianki recalls
near the end of his story. "How can we bring them back to
life?" old man Bianki asks in his child's voice. What you
need are some good, strong words. "What you need is poetry":
that unwieldy, cardboard word he carried around all his life,
to no avail.

Before he discovered ornithology, the young boy was driven
on another sort of hunt—soccer. He played for the storied

clubs Petrovsky, Neva, Unitas. He was the winner, incidentally, of the Saint Petersburg season trophy for 1913. The season trophy—in April the wind from the Neva fills with the scent of dun-colored, crumbling ice. Rostral beauties raise to the wind their buoyant, erect nipples.

Tall for his age, wearing gaiters, with a sweaty forehead and gritty, salty hair, the adolescent Bianki pursues the ball: His breathing grows sharp, with the occasional pleasurable ache.

His father, a famous ornithologist, the very one after whom the young boy trotted along the large-windowed, empty halls of the museum, did not approve of soccer—he wanted to see in his son a replica of himself, naturally. His son obediently enrolled in the natural sciences section of the Department of Physics and Mathematics at Petrograd University, but he never finished, since things finished of their own accord.

COLD-BLOODED?

Almost a graduate, almost a poet, almost a scholar. "People touched by fire are sensitive, fragile." Those touched by fire, Shvarts observed, not wanting to miss any chance to observe, and those abandoned on the ice.

Now what should/shall I do? Stop dead? Go quiet?

Encased in ice, shall I pretend to be ice? Take the form of the coming winter? Freeze over, like a frozen dream: In the white-pink night the river Fontanka flows like tomato juice from a broken jar into a puddle, when actually it's your hands covered in blood. And I, who up to this moment have accompanied you at a delicately maintained distance and with re-SPECT-ful aloofness, bow down to lick those idiotic bloody smashed huge fingers. Fighting off drunken surprise, you sternly say, "That doesn't give you the right to use the familiar with me."

Yes—I think I'll pretend to be ice.

Bianki himself, by the way, writes magical (that is, good and strong and useful) words about turning to ice. He spits on the end of his stubby pencil and writes not poetry but the diary of a naturalist. The onset of autumn chill he depicts either as torture or as the act of love, there's no distinguishing: "The winds—reapers of leaves—tear the last rags from the forest. Having accomplished its first task—undressing the forest—autumn sets about its second task: making the water colder and colder. Fish crowd into deep crannies to winter where the water won't turn to ice. Cold blood freezes even on dry land. Insects, mice, spiders, centipedes hide themselves away. Snakes crawl into dry holes, wind around each other, and go still. Frogs push into the mud, lizards hide under the last bark left on the tree stumps and enter a trance. Outside there are seven kinds of weather: It tosses, blows, shatters, blinds, howls, pours, and sweeps up from the ground."

    To become a motionless snake curling up against other motionless snakes, to hibernate—that is my task today. The leaf-reaping season is one you can survive, can overcome, only by metamorphosis: by changing your nature so you become part of the background, be it snow, dirt, or night.

## A TUNNEL AND A CERTAIN SOMEONE

How can you make out white against white? Bianki hoped he could see it, while hoping others couldn't see him. Now for perhaps his most terrifying fairy tale.

### MR. FOX AND MOUSIE

Mousie-mouse, why is your nose so black?
I was digging in the dirt.
Why were you digging in the dirt?
I made myself a burrow.
Why did you make yourself a burrow?
To hide, Mr. Fox, from you!
Mousie-mouse, I'll keep watch at your door!
Oh, I've a soft bed in my burrow.
You'll have to eat—then out you'll sneak!
Oh, I've a cupboard in my burrow.
Mousie-mouse, I'll dig up your burrow!
Oh, I'll run down a little tunnel—
And off he goes!

It's probable Bianki was arrested by organs of the Soviet secret police more often than most of his literary colleagues— a total of five (5) times. Five (5) times in a row he repeated the drill: the awful wait for the inevitable, the awful relief when the awful event itself begins, the humiliation, the hopelessness, the hope, the despair, the weeks and months of paralysis, the miracle.

A local historian who got access to the archives reports:

> While digging around in the files of the archive of the former regional committee of the Soviet Communist Party, I came across an interesting document completely by accident—a summary of charges written up on February 23, 1925, by the Altai office of the State Political Directorate to bring to trial a group of Socialist Revolutionaries living in Barnaul and Biisk. (All of them had arrived "from Russia," as they said back then.) It included several references to Vitaly Bianki. They are:
>
> In November 1918, there arrived in Biisk one Belianin-Bianki Vitaly Valentinovich, an SR and writer for the SR newspaper *The People*, who was active in the Committee on Education and who around that time, fearing Kolchak's reprisals, changed his real name from Bianki to Belianin. Said Belianin-Bianki, upon arriving in Biisk with his wife, Zinaida Alexandrovna Zakharovich, stayed at the apartment of local SR and member of the Constituent Assembly, Liubimov, Nikolai Mikhailovich. It was through him that Belianin-Bianki began to make contact with the local SR organization . . . He entered the employ of the Biisk Agricultural Board as a clerk of the second class . . .
>
> In 1921 the Cheka in Biisk arrested him twice. In addition, he was imprisoned as a hostage for three weeks.
>
> In September 1922 V. Bianki received word of pending arrest and, on the pretext of a business trip, left for Petrograd with his family.

At the end of 1925 Bianki was again arrested and sentenced to three years' exile in Uralsk for belonging to a nonexistent underground organization. In 1928 (thanks to constant petitioning by, among others, Gorky, who approached Cheka chief Yagoda) he received permission to move to Novgorod, and then to Leningrad. In November 1932 came another arrest. After three and a half weeks he was released "for lack of evidence." In March 1935 Bianki, as "the son of a non-hereditary nobleman, a former SR, an active participant in armed resistance to Soviet power," was again arrested and sentenced to exile for five years in the Aktiubinsk region. It was only thanks to E. P. Peshkova's intervention that his sentence was commuted and Bianki was freed.

The bulk of his fairy tales are about the hunt and the chase, about deadly danger and struggle.

But what's most striking is his tone: Not a trace of sentimentality, no sympathy for the preyed-upon or the fallen. Each death, each act of cruelty, belongs to the natural order.

"If you kill a bird with a metal ring on its leg, remove the ring and send it to a tagging center. If you catch a bird with a ring, write down the letters and numbers stamped on the ring. If not you but another hunter or bird catcher you know kills or captures such a bird, tell him what he needs to do." No pity for anyone; the hunter is always justified in his desire to master and seize and sacrifice a life—and turn it into a mounted specimen. Every victim gets his chance to escape, says Bianki, and it's a sorry fool who doesn't see it and grab it.

## A GUST OF WIND

At first all of these words and shadows of birds and fish, and
the giant with the voice of a munchkin, were indistinct forms
inside me, and when they first took shape, they looked like
this (autumn was just ending, and in the Amherst dusk you
could hear all around the moaning of owls arrived en masse
from God knows where):

> The massive-awesome Bacchus Bianki
> thrusts fat fingers into ominous cracks in the
> frozen earth, and from there (from where)
> he harvests miracle-solace-refuse-sense,
> tipsy sober timid bombastic, he knows each
> tangled root, and he writes like he ransacks.
> The stilling forest thrusts the wind's damp
> shag down his throat—the black box
> of night sky on the verge of winter.
> .........................................
> Ready for first frost are you now yourself?
> Ready for first frost are you now an owl?
> Ready for first frost are you now a widow?

Here the author dozes off, and the owls, too. The author
dreams of the other author's poem:

> The wind roared up the riverbank,
> drove waves upon the shore—
> its furious whistle gave a scare
> to a red-throated loon.

It knocked the magpie from the grove,
spun and dropped into the waves—
there it took a giant gulp
and choked, and down it dove.

The thing he did best was tracking birds.

## NOTES OF AN ORNITHOLOGIST

Why Vitaly Bianki went to Leningrad during the blockade, how he ended up there—the explanations we have don't make sense. Either he went to bring food to his Leningrad friends or he was trying to get food from his Leningrad friends (both versions astonish), or he went just to have a look, or to make an appearance, or to punish himself. When he returned, he lay down and did not get up.

This is what his diary entries show:

> April 6: Stayed in bed.
> April 7: Stayed in bed.
> April 8: Stayed in bed.

Nevertheless, everything he had heard-seen he described well and concealed (meaning, up to the day of his death) well. I am prepared to state that among those who visited during the blockade, the naturalist-dilettante Bianki turned out to be the best-qualified and most perceptive and methodical witness: what was impossible to look at, he examined and categorized. Nevertheless, his notebooks

—fully published now—have not, of course, found their reader.

They've winged past us like yet another repulsive salvo from 1941—one today's readers try to duck as frantically as their unfortunate predecessors tried to duck shells on Leningrad's streets, so visible and familiar to the German pilot.

Bianki—an unsuccessful, unrealized scholar, but a scholar nonetheless—organized his impressions under phenomeno-logical rubrics: blockade style, blockade humor, blockade consciousness, blockade smile, blockade language, blockade cityscape, blockade femininity, blockade Jews. This is to say that in two weeks he understood what we have yet to for-mulate for ourselves—that the blockade was a unique civi-lization with the characteristic features of all human societies.

> This is how they smile here.
> This is how they barter here.
> This how they fear, and no longer fear.

This is how they joke here, and it is this subject—which is curious and handy for our script—which brings them to-gether: Bianki quotes Shvarts as one of the best blockade humorists. Since we know that Shvarts left the city in De-cember, we may conclude that his jokes lingered in the city into spring—they didn't melt (in general, nothing in that city melted).

Yes, here they meet—two utterly different storytellers on the Leningrad scene, two magic wizards and didacts. The one had a bear and a dragon, the other had fireflies, titmice, shrews—all metaphors for blockade life. The writers themselves were transformed by the era into clowning yarnspinners forced to camouflage their brutal and piquant observations about human nature.

Shvarts the blockade jokester eventually produced the most important book we have on the phenomenon of "Leningrad literature of the mid-Soviet period"—his "phone book" (variously, his "inventory"), a *Kunstkamera* of spiritual deformities and disasters. Among the era's victims is a cardiologist listed under the letter "D," a man with hideously burned hands. His patient Shvarts, seeing those two pink, tender, shining hands, reflects: "During an experiment an oxygen tank exploded, the door was jammed, and he forced open the burning panels with his bare hands. They were so badly burned that he almost lost them. He was considered one of the best cardiologists in the city. He was beaten to death for reasons far removed from science, but whether there were parts of his soul as deformed as the skin on his hands—I could not discern." That's precisely what he wanted to do—to discern, to see inside.

It turns out the blockade was the main event of Shvarts's life in Leningrad—though the whole time he intended, he prepared himself, to speak about the Terror, his main chosen task. He kept being swept toward the blockade winter that followed the Terror—he couldn't control himself, couldn't help speaking about it. For him that winter illuminated and explained everything and everyone, whereas the recent purges had made everything confused and unclear. Almost every topic, every figure, every character in his "phone book" reminds him of that winter, drags him back there. He remembers roofs, bombs, bomb shelters, the faces and conversations of his neighbors in the dark, and, most of all, his failed intention to write it all down, right then and there, in the wake of words just spoken—his failed play, in which he tried to render his strongest impression, the endless blockade night: "We descended to the bottom of the cagelike staircase and stood in a corner like a coven of witches, while the planes and their mechanical-animal whine would not relent, they circled and circled and with every pass dropped bombs. Then antiaircraft fire—and when it hits its mark, there's a dry pop, and the smooth tin bird flaps its tin wings."

Only in this avian metaphor will their visions of the blockade coincide: Bianki calls his blockade notes "City Abandoned by Birds." For him that's a euphemism, dialect for a curse, his "no" to hope.

Shvarts's notebook was an act of mourning for his play, which never quite happened. But from his notebook's scattered, roughly stitched-together human plots the blockade emerges as the true home for the soul of the Leningrad intellectual who lived through the '30s. In other words, it was hell, the only vale where the coward-soul, slave-soul, traitor-soul, the soul in constant pain, never and nowhere not in pain, might abide—those Leningrad writer-survivors who, in front of the witnessing Shvarts, go out of their minds (then later, reluctantly, taking their time, come back into their minds), faint as noiselessly as leaves on exiting the torture chamber of Party hearings, and continually hone their skill at slander. Shvarts buried, escorted off, and lost one by one all of his titans, his cherished enemies (nothing matches the white heat of his elegiac and erotic hatred-passion for Oleinikov).

All he saw around him now were Voevodins, Rysses, and Azarovs and other small fry stomped on by the century: these characters were relieved to find themselves in the blockade—what he called, narrowing his eyes, a *benign* calamity, the kind that kills you without implicating you.

Can we say that for Bianki, too, the blockade was a benign calamity?

Apparently there is a phenomenon called "precipitous birth"— the infant bursts into the world through a mother who has had no time to get accustomed to that degree of pain.

The precipitous blockade of someone who visits the city suddenly and briefly is the precipitous birth of knowledge. He sees everything—not accustomed to the situation, not fused with it, he does not experience the slow, daily disappearance of meaning and God. On the wings of an airplane (which he immediately compared to a bird, Bianki was incapable of doing otherwise), he is transported to a place of blank, universal desolation—until then, he had only heard of it from the pitiful, apologetic letters of his dying Leningrad friends.

Shvarts's interest in the blockade was people, preferably the extras (the big stars for the most part nimbly made tracks to the east during the warm months of the year): children, old ladies, custodians, luckless local officials, and spies, almost none of whom would live until spring.

But Bianki, hounded from childhood by the word "poetry," is interested in metaphors, namely, hybrid monsters: birds and fish fused with planes, fireflies joined with phosphorous

metal in the night sky. How do fragments of blockade existence camouflage themselves, what forms do they assume?
Here the blockade becomes a natural phenomenon, a kind
of *Naturphilosophie* of the blockade world emerges. From
the very first impression, everything looks unnatural: the
plane's wings, unlike those of Bianki's bluethroats and star-
lings, are rigid—and the plane isn't even a bird but a fish, an
aerial fish. Monstrous specimen!

All this he tries to discern in the blockade city—and can't
find the direct words for (for which reason, most likely, he
subsequently falls ill), so he reconstitutes it metaphorically.
The dead city revives, pretends it's animate—like a museum
diorama: "The city spreads out around us farther and farther.
Slowly, as in a slow-motion film, slowly people wander. Not
people: monkeys with noses. Especially the women: boney
faces, caverns for cheeks—unbelievably sharp, elongated
noses…"

As it was with that diorama from childhood, it's impossible
to make out what's dead and what's alive, what is a monkey
with a nose and what is a deformed blockade soul caricatured
by dystrophy.

On returning from the dead city, he wrote down an awful
little poem, as often happened with him in moments of
agitation—the words just spilled out:

> Unbearable: the cold like a wolf,
> A growing list of deprivations,
> A hammer going in my temples:
> There people are dying, dying in vain!

## WAGTAILS. THE LANGUAGE OF BIRDS

On returning from the dead city, he had a good long rest, scratched out something in his secret diary, and again took to walking deep into the forest and just standing there—his eyes open sometimes and sometimes shut, listening hard, sniffing, studying. The world Bianki inhabited is alien to us; his words are obscure and hence alluring, and they unsettle us even as they speak to us:

"Bluethroats and brightly colored stonechats have appeared in the wet bushes, and golden wagtails in the swamps. Pink-breasted fiscals (shrikes) are here, with thick ruffs of feathers, and the land rail, the corncrake, the blue-green roller have returned from distant parts."

So tell me—what are all these creatures? What do we picture as we follow the phrase "the pink-breasted shrikes," what sort of impossible, absurd marvels? It is perfectly obvious—perfect and obvious—that the author invented them all. Displayed before us is some other planet born from the imagination of a man who could not come up with a persuasive reason to inhabit his own.

Wagtails? What do you mean, wagtails? No, you're wrong, Bianki insists, that's us living on our planet, in our swamp—alien, blind, speechless, bereft.

We (meaning I) are not familiar with the bluethroat (bird of the thrush family, sparrow genus). Depending on classificatory approach, it may, along with all varieties of nightingale, be ascribed to the family of flycatchers. In size somewhat smaller than the domestic sparrow. Body length about 15 centimeters. Weight of male is 15 to 23 grams, female 13 to 21 grams. Spine light brown or gray-brown, tail feathers reddish. Throat and crop blue with reddish spot in the center; the spot may also be white or bordered with white. The blue color edged underneath first with black, then with red half circles across the breast. Tail red with black sheen, middle pair of tail feathers light brown. Female has neither blue nor red coloring. Throat whitish, bordered with a brown half circle. Bill black, legs black-brown.

Whatever the throat and the crop look like, when you descend into this prose, you descend into an invented, crafted world. The further you proceed into that roller-and-green-azure language, the less you hear the waves striking University Embankment, and the more the whole hysteria-hypocrisy of the city—with its literati stinging one another and raising glasses of poison, and its ultraliterary footbridges—fades into the distance. Bianki remains, just Bianki, stepping through the slush of the frozen swamp, listening with his whole being—here you have the voices of birds, you have the voices of fish. That very same fairy-tale dunce who, scrambling to hide from the tsar, ran into a grove and suddenly understood the language of the forest. "I hope to create an explanatory dictionary of the language of local places." Places not of this world! In periodic self-imposed exile in the village of Mikheevo in the Moshensky region, where he landed-hid during that first winter of the war, he does not stop collecting the magical words that protect him: a hidden, invisible language, a collection of real words—his article of faith.

## A HAPPY ENDING

"Our forest correspondents cleared the ice from the bottom of a local pond and dug up the silt. In the silt there were a number of frogs who had gathered there in heaps for the winter. When they pulled them out, they were like pure glass. Their bodies had grown extremely brittle. Their tiny legs would snap from the slightest, faintest touch, and did so with a light, clear pop. Our forest correspondents took several of the frogs home with them. They carefully warmed up the frozen juvenile frogs in their heated rooms. The frogs came to life bit by bit and began hopping across the floor."

And off they go!

# LIVING PICTURES
*A Fairy-Tale Document*

CHARACTERS
*Antonina "Totya" (thirty-seven years old)*
*Moisei (twenty-five years old)*
*Anna Pavlovna, a supervisor at the Hermitage (seventy years old)*

SCENE ONE: LITTLE BUNDLES. NOVEMBER.

*(A table stands on a semidark stage. On the table two people try to find room, arrange themselves. They are Moisei and Totya. Both are wrapped in dirty-white quilted bedcovers and whatever else comes to hand. Slowly the audience's eyes grow accustomed to the dim lighting, and it becomes apparent that the action takes place in one of the halls of the Hermitage. The floor is covered with broken glass and sand.)*

T: You know, my dear friend . . . I'm fucking freezing!

*(Moisei and Totya flop around, trying to get closer, clumsily; their movements are reminiscent of seals on a beach.)*

M: Is that better?
T: Now I'm even colder . . .

M: All right, now what?

T: (*quietly*) I'm afraid...

M: Say what? Totya! Totya! What did you say? (*Since Moisei is wrapped in a comforter and has several scarves and a knitted cap on his head, he can't hear very well. In general, their habit of calling each other's names, of calling out to each other, is important.*)

T: Goddammit, Musya, my very dearest, I'm afraid! I'm A-FRAID!

M: Totya, don't shout, please ... and don't curse. I don't like it. I love you—but I can't stand the way you talk! And don't complain—you can't keep up a good attitude like that ... We agreed not to whine. And I thought you were never afraid. Remember when Irakly introduced us: "Moisei, may I introduce you to Totya, who has graced us with her presence—the most beautiful woman in Leningrad ... And the most daring—she conquers mountains and hearts!"

T: He didn't say "the most shameless"?

M: That goes without saying.

T: (*playing it up*) "Virginal Moisei, may I introduce you to the conqueror of mountains, and of the most bulging crotches and unassailable zippers! Mount Elbruses of male vanity and lust! Compiler of the most intriguing sexual record in the City of Three Revolutions..."

M: Totya, don't be crude! I'll fine you—every time! ... I'll make you pay ... for each bad word—one kiss!

T: Well, of course, as many as you want—I was afraid you'd start demanding cigarettes or candy or something ... my sweet little caramels ... but a kiss—no problem, except every time I'll have to unwrap you ... and then rewrap you. So I'll be unwrapping and rewrapping endlessly...

M: That's right, I'm going to demand kisses! Otherwise we'll stop having feelings in this hell and start acting like animals! We're already becoming animals... (*Excited/upset, he raises himself, loses his balance and tumbles/slides off the table.*)

T: Moisei!

(*A pause. Silence.*)

T: Musya...where are you? Where are you? Did you fall? Did you slide off? Are you hurt? I can't see you!

(*Moisei half laughs and half whimpers on the floor.*)

T: Moisei, are you okay? Where are you? (*She has a coughing fit.*)

M: Yes...I was just thinking, I slid off inside my cocoon and now I'm like our favorite mummy in the Egyptian gallery—the priest mummy! 1000 BC, in satisfactory condition.

T: You know, when I was younger people would visit that exhibit and kept saying the name "Fall-i-set." I could never remember that word. At first, whenever I looked at him, I thought, why does he have that full lip, that salacious look—I always imagined he was laughing at me...when Masha was arrested and then released...and when Irakly was arrested and released...and when Papa was arrested and released, and then arrested again...So now he's laughing at all of us...He's a mummy and we've all...become... like him...we'll become...(*She suddenly pauses hard.*)

M: Totya? Did you stop? Don't stop! I'm afraid when there's no sound...What is this, first she's quiet, then she's cursing...

T: "Fall-i-sets"... That's exactly what they call them now...

M: Call who? Where? What are you talking about?

T: I heard it from that, you know, our building manager... truly disgusting face, I should say... unbelievably disgusting! He's stuffed it full. The sanitation workers who pick them up call them bundles, and mummies, and you know what else—get ready for this—flowers... they call them... snowdrops...

M: Flowers? Why flowers?

T: They get left... at hospitals... entryways... under streetlights—in rags and blankets with loud colors, so you can find them... And the workers call them "flowers"... They say, "Time to pick the flowers..."

M: My God! But what do snowdrops have to do with it?

T: You have no imagination... When spring arrives: it all creeps out from under the snow, you can see everything... Though what am I saying, what spring?—it's been snowing since October.

M: It's amazing, Totya, these new expressions, like the siege had its own language...

T: Its own language, its own habits, its own values, its own laws...

M: Yes, and its own style!

*(Moisei finally manages to sit upright under the comforter and undo himself, to free himself, and we see that he's wrapped in whatever he could find: scarves, some sort of jacket, a strange old-fashioned woman's cap; on his hands there's a muff, which he looks at fixedly, amazed...)*

M: Yes... if someone had said to me a year ago that I'd be sitting with my love, my own true love, wearing a lady's cap and muff... I'd be... I'd really be very surprised! Are you listening, sweetie? It wasn't often I went to a tryst in a muff and a bonnet.

T: Fact is, you didn't go to many trysts... Moisei, how did you even find it, that muff?

M: Totya, you're jealous... jealous of me? How strangely gratifying!

T: God no... jealous... no... I'm just thinking... about when I first heard the word "muff," how it got stuck in my head. Mama would read us that story about the Snow Queen—me and Masha... You remember that book?

M: The yellow one, Ganzen's translation? Oh, I even remember how it smelled! Books smell so good...

T: (*declaiming in a "child's" loud voice*) Gerda and she got into the sleigh and raced across stumps and hillocks into a thicket of trees. The little robber girl was Gerda's height but much stronger, bigger in the shoulders, and dark-skinned. Her eyes were completely black but somehow sad. She hugged Gerda and said, "They won't kill you, as long as you don't make me angry! You're a princess, right?"

"No!" Gerda answered, and explained what she had been through and how she loved Kay.

The little robber girl looked at her very seriously, nodded her head and said, "They won't kill you even if I do get mad at you—but it would be better if I killed you right now!" She wiped away Gerda's tears and then buried her hands in a beautiful, soft, warm muff.

M: And here I am hiding my skin and bones in this lovely muff... which is, by the way, totally moth-eaten... kind of disgusting... But how do you remember that so well? How do you know it by heart?

T: Oh! That was my favorite game with Masha! We always

acted out fairy tales...and, of course..."The Snow Queen"...That was our favorite: We were so scared by all that dead beauty. We would act it out—we called it living pictures from Andersen...tableaux vivants...We did it every evening...But I never knew who to play, I wanted to be every one of them: the little robber girl, Gerda, the Snow Queen. (*She tries to depict them as she names them.*) I understood them all, you know? As a girl I somehow thought that each of them was me, and I was all of them... and then Masha started to sing...she thought up a song... and was always singing the Queen's song. (*She sings the melody, but stumbles; Moisei tries to pick it up, but completely off-key.*)

M: No, Totya, the little robber girl is exactly who you are now...You're always cursing at me, losing your temper, any minute now you'll start a fight...

T: (*as though thinking aloud, speaking to herself*) I always used to wonder...the Snow Queen: Is she bad or good? Evil or kind? Will she kill him or save him? (*In an icy voice she performs the Snow Queen.*) I will no longer kiss you! Or I will kiss you to death!

M: Totya, come kiss me! Don't you know we're having a TRYST!...We are having a rendezvous, my love, nobody else is here, Totya. All those gloomy wraiths are down there in the bomb shelter...

T: Silly boy, what are we going to do at a rendezvous like this?

M: I want to read to you from my diary, I want to smoke a cigarette with you, there are all kinds of things I want to do...if you can just help me...mmm...with the unwrapping...

T: Musya, we don't have any light, though we do have eczema, gingivitis, bloody diarrhea ... What kind of rendezvous is this?

M: Well, we've got some oil cake, some burned sugar and coffee grounds ... And no one else is here, my dear Antonina Nikolaevna, we are alone at last! How nice—nobody around, living or dead!

T: No big difference! And, Musya, please don't sound so confident ... It's not that clear what category we belong to ...

M: Madame Tonya, you're wrong!

T: (*irritated and puzzled*) What's going on? Why are you getting formal on me?

M: I have a Dear Totya and a Madame Totya ... You know, when I see you as a small, sweet angry child, then you're Dear Totya, and when you're huge and forbidding, then you're Madame ...

T: It doesn't matter, there's no difference ... it doesn't matter now.

M: Tonya, you're wrong! We're alive, we're in the category of the living, and our ration cards are in the worker category! We'll just hope those bastards don't dare fire us to save rations ... right now we are alive ... and I don't see it, how can we possibly die?

T: Well, everyone around us is dying ... And they used to be alive and talked just like you ... Have you gone out into the city? Have you looked? Have you seen *them* laid out on the ice? Everywhere!

M: Stop! I see you, I hear you ... I hear you breathing ... I hear you walking! When I hear that, I know everything's still ahead of us! This is just the beginning ...

T: (*damping his pathos*) Well, my breathing isn't so great: Just listen ... this stupid cold! Just listen. (*She takes a breath.*)

M: You breathe so beautifully, Totya...You breathe beautifully, better than anyone! Everything's just beginning, I know it!

T: That was before, when we were reading fortunes in the coffee grounds, Musya, and now we're eating the grounds ...and consider it a privilege! Why is that? Because we don't dare read fortunes anymore...We don't dare think about the future...

M: (*proud, stubborn*) Everything's just beginning...I'm telling you!

T: For you everything's just beginning, but I'm thirty-seven years old...compared to me you're a child...my boy... the artist...

M: I'm not a boy, I'm a man! Will you take me as a husband, Tonechka? We're a perfect match: he's a boy-artist, she's an art historian, a lady critic: I'll splash paint around, and you'll praise me, so my name won't disappear from the annals of history...(*in a flirtatious, capricious-pleading tone*) Antonina Nikolaevna, will you marry me?

T: You're no husband, you're a boy! Don't ask such silly questions, or I'll roll you back up!

*(Totya very slowly starts transforming/wrapping Moisei into a "cocoon," softly and hoarsely singing under her breath, as though she were rocking him to sleep.)*

## SCENE TWO: PICTURE FRAMES. DECEMBER.

M: Who's there? Who is it?

T: It's nice that no one's here, Moisei...(*Dreamy, languorous.*) You know what we'll do now?

M: Mmm, yes?

T: Talk about Masha's soup...

M: But we have a rule not to do that! We can't talk about Masha's soup! That's not allowed, absolutely not, love! It's a good way to get depressed!

T: Mmmmm, haricots verts soup, beans floating around in it and little orange circles of fat, I just kept touching them with my spoon...

M: Fine! We agreed we wouldn't talk about food, only about afterwards—I really want to talk about afterwards, Totya! About when all this has passed...when it's over...

T: Musya, what are you saying, you don't understand—what "afterwards"? This will never end!...I count every day but this never ends...Yesterday was day one hundred...I thought they might announce it on the radio, but they just go on about the same thing—victorious battles and the defenders' valor. Don't look here, look over there!

M: Totya, everything passes—and this will pass. I'll slap together a thousand amazing paintings for you, simple ones, scary ones, gorgeous ones, ugly ones...Whatever kind you like—and you'll like them all...You'll have a good laugh!

T: (teasing) You really think I'll like them all?

M: Well, that was probably dumb...But now and then you'll like one...you'll look at them with your icy blue eyes and speak in that stern icy tone! Your voice will tinkle slightly... like the icicles in the bomb shelter..."This one was a waste of time, Moisei, this you just...farted out!"

T: It doesn't matter if you "fart it out"—I'll praise you, I'll praise you to everyone! I'll be so proud of you.

M: I know what your praise sounds like...I remember how you praised Picasso when we first met. "Do you know, Moisei, he fucking captures things whole!..."

T: And what was I supposed to say—I don't have other words, my love, for what he does!...

*(She trails off. In the darkness someone moves past holding an oil lamp. All you can see is a flame "walking." Totya and Moisei watch intently.)*

"THE FLAME": (*a little hoarsely-shrilly*) Agh! Who's there?
M *and* T: Who's there?
AP: Antonina Nikolaevna! Dearie, what are you doing here? Why aren't you in the bomb shelter? I just don't understand you! (*She examines them and their quarters.*) You're going to freeze here! You know, it's more comfortable there... more sociable...
T: More sociable?! You've got some thirty-two people sociably dying there...
M: Totinka don't, not now...Don't talk about that—it upsets you...
T: (*in a stubborn, frightening, lifeless voice, on the verge of hysteria*) And Sonya, and Olga Petrovna, and red-haired Kolya, and gray-haired Kolya, and Irakly...Irakly...
M: Totya, don't torture yourself! Don't talk about them!
T: (*coughing/laughing, now with rising hysteria*) Irakly tells me: "Totya, do you remember when you hung Cézanne's *Blue Apples* next to the window? I was furious at you!..." He said that and stopped...and I said, "You, Irakly, are a conceited ass! There's light there: the color coming from the window, from the Neva, is blue! Do you really not see it? Do you not see anything with regard to color?..." And he said, "And what do you understand, you idiot, about how blue light moves. Look, see how it falls here, and

here ... but not there ..." That's what he said, (*dragging it out*) iiii—diiii-ot ...

AP: Well, I have to say, dearie, you shouldn't do that! You'll magnify the colors ...

T: I don't magnify them! The light falls or it doesn't ... But I probably was being an idiot. My nanny used to say, "Where others have gone, Ton'ka's gone wrong."

AP: What are you saying, Antonina Nikolaevna ... Take our Adrian Leonidovich, what a wonderful, wonderful man! He's doesn't give up, he's invented the best imaginable stove! Just think, he was inspired by the sixteenth-century Dutch stove—the subject of his dissertation, by the way ...

T: Sometimes I think we're burying ourselves in the past, we're using sixteenth-century stoves, and Moisei here writes away in his little diary, even though he can't see a thing, he's like a blind mole, his hands are almost gone, but he keeps scratching away by torchlight. He calls it "Diary of a Caveman" ... And you, Anna Pavlovna, which cave are you headed for now?

AP: (*a little embarrassed, but stubbornly proud*) I'm, you know, going to see him ...

T AND M: (*in loud amusement*) Rembrandt again?

T: But those halls are empty, completely empty... Aren't you afraid, Anna Pavlovna? Why do you go by yourself?

AP: How can you even ask, dearie? You think these paintings have lived here for centuries and suddenly they don't exist because of some evacuation? Because of this cursed blockade? I've spent fifty years with them, I know their every crease ... every crease! As if the war could make anything go away! You should know better: It's all here ... everything is here—you just need to be able to see and remember how to see! You know, my dears, whenever anyone comes, I tell them about the paintings.

M: (*reviving a bit*) Oh! People come here?

AP: Of course they do! Just yesterday a lovely young man from the Baltic Fleet came to check the electrical system … can you believe, he took some macaroni from his pocket … nice cooked macaroni … and put it in my mouth … like this. (*She demonstrates on Tonya, getting a little embarrassed about just how he did it.*) And, you know, by then I really wasn't feeling well. Not well at all. In return I took him to the Danaë and showed him everything!

T: (*lighting up a cigarette*) You showed the Danaë's everything to the generous young sailor? … Ooh la la!

M: Tonya, come on! So what do you mean—you showed her? She was evacuated over the Urals! Orbeli sent her off first thing!

AP: You know, I just … told him about her! From memory. I mean, I'll always remember everything about her … I remember them all … They're still here, you know. (*She points to her eyes and into the darkness.*)

M: So, why the Danaë? Why the Danaë, exactly?

AP: Well, I just thought a young man would like her—she's so wonderfully golden, so warm … Now everyone's cold, but she's warm! Though you yourselves know, there are paintings more in tune with my emotional state … his old men, his old women …

T: Anna Pavlovna! *Putain!* What emotional state?! The Danaë, she's … life … yes, she's life itself … She's the only one you should be telling about …

M: Well, I would have told him about the Prodigal Son …

T: Why? Why would he want to hear that?

M: I'm always glad he came back, you know... I'm glad for all
of them... that they met again at last—and I think about
the father... You know I always think about how back there
they... may be worrying. (*He blows his nose, protractedly.*)

(*Out of the darkness descend/appear picture frames. They glim-
mer with a dull, warm golden light. Each of the characters
appears captured in a gleaming frame. Each begins his mono-
logue in the "professional" tone of a tour guide, at once ecstatic
and robotic, and then gradually grows more animated, turns
into a hybrid of himself and Rembrandt's subject.*)

AP: The Hermitage's collection of Rembrandt van Rijn, the
great Dutch master, is one of the museum's treasures. It
boasts more than twenty canvases. Every period of his
career is represented. The name of the man depicted in
*Portrait of an Elderly Man in Red*, like the names of many
of his models during the years 1650 to 1660, is unknown.
While the individual features of those depit... (*she stumbles trying to say the difficult word*) de-pict-ed are preserved,
they are unified by a single theme—a meditation on the
meaning of life and death... (*Here she begins to change
from a guide-robot into herself, as if waking up, and she hits
her stride.*) Rembrandt is attracted by the faces of older
people... Rembrandt's old men and women! What have
they learned? What do they see ahead? What are their
thoughts? The face of an old man, a face covered in wrinkles—wrinkles of weariness, calm, understanding, ac-
ceptance... He is very tired. Yes, yes... I am very tired.
Yes, he is very tired. His face gleams out of the darkness,
against fabric the color of bordeaux, the color of blood...

His hands are clasped. Clasped like this. Aged hands that know everything! He's no longer afraid of anything. He gets more and more afraid! (*Plaintively*) He still hasn't achieved anything, he's only beginning to understand, only beginning to see . . . And all this—the terror and the hope—is expressed in his hands, his remarkable hands! . . .

M: That's so true, such remarkable hands . . . The hands of the old man, the father's hands, placed on his son's shoulder! Totya! Anna Pavlovna! Look at this . . . (*Anna Pavlovna makes gestures showing that he needs to be more serious, and he draws himself up and continues.*) *The Return of the Prodigal Son*—Rembrandt's highest achievement! Before us we see the famous biblical tale: The prodigal son is shown covered in scars; he has traveled the earth in search of happiness, glory, heroic deeds, wealth, pleasure, but he lost everything . . . I would even say he lost himself . . . His back trembling with anguish and humiliation, he kneels before his father. His whole back expresses shame and grief, but the father's face is peaceful and soft with compassion! His aging hands, his fingers, tremble with happiness—at embracing his son again, touching him, catching his scent, pulling him close. For him the work of forgiveness is easy. They lean against each other with hope for the future . . . expecting . . . they will have a future . . .

T: The Royal Danaë: She's pure expectation! The picture's very composition, the arrangement of the heavy folds of the drapery, details like the little table at the head of her bed or the elegant shoes dropped from her feet—these are techniques of the Dutch genre masters. With Rembrandt such details acquire special significance . . . significance. (What am I saying . . . what significance . . . where did I get these words?) The Royal Danaë is nervous ... the tips of her fingers are ... shaking. (*Looks at her own hands, then at Moisei.*) Why are they shaking? From fear? From desire? From joy at meeting her lover? At meeting her future? The princess's glowing face is hidden in shadow, turned to the light: the Danaë is resisting the dark of imprisonment. She wants to flee the darkness. Her huge golden body is turned toward the window, anticipating her fate. She radiates warmth, and she feels warm! But I'm cold, Moisei! What are we doing, what does any of this have to do with us? (*She gets out of the frame as though she'd suddenly woken from a dream, or vision.*)

AP: They have to do with everyone, dearie! And it will always be like that ... always ... even afterwards: It's so important to know that someone will exist in that *afterwards.* (*She finds a rag-as-handkerchief and blows into it for a long time.*) You know, me and Sonya, Sofiya Evgenievna, God forgive us, have been going to look at the still lifes ... we get up and think ... we stand there and look at them ... and it's painful but, you know, it's also good ... so you enjoy yourself now and then ... God forgive us ... Rubens, you know, looks very good to me now—all those carcasses, cheeses, fruits ... yes, the cheeses ... and sugar ... hunks of sugar ... and bread ...

T: Uh-huh, and our Irakly even started writing verses—about the edible Hermitage ... He'd eat his oil cake, sip some boiled water, and start moaning ... describing still lifes, I mean ...

M: Oh, oh, this is my favorite one ... (*He checks his memory. He frees his hand from its wrappings and gesticulates as he recites.*)

SNYDERS

A watermelon glows a bloody red,
The tender fat of lamb roasts gleams,
The primal ocean's marvels spread,
They quiver and display their sheen.

Homer, Shakespeare of the table,
Who worships more the "lifeless thing"?
Joyful Snyders calls us to the revel,
And every person feels his hunger sing:

On seeing the amber bunch of fruit,
The succulent pear, the pistachio nut,
The sfumato of plums and lemon's sunset.

But once my eyes have had their feast,
Dear Snyders, I only wish (God's least)
I had your still life to digest.

(*Laughs sadly.*) What a sad irony, sweetheart! The great
Snyders and this damned, pathetic, humiliating hunger...
T: Musya, you shouldn't be thinking about this, you aren't
allowed! And enough of this remembering poor Irakly
and his fits of ecstasy—he and his "lemon's sunset" have
been cooling off downstairs for how many days?...We
had an agreement—no talking about food! Akh, Anna
Pavlovna, why did you get us started? Why are we making
all this up? What kind of game is this? Why paint all
these wonders? It a lie, for fuck's sake! What sfumato?
We're dystrophics, let's talk about that—and no mincing

words…How about I read you something…something…
like this…(*She reads in a terrifying voice at Anna Pavlovna, at Moisei, and at the audience, in turn.*)

ROO-ROO

I'm stupid, I'm shit, I'm a cripple,
I'd kill a man for a tipple.
Let us in, we're at the door,
We scrabble like wild dogs.
You butchers, I'm in pain
From awful bladder strain!

AP: Don't do that! I don't want to hear it! Don't you dare
do that around me! Don't you dare!
T: (*yells, snarls at her*) Roo! Roo! That's how it really is! That,
darling, is how it is…(*Cries.*)

(*Anna Pavlovna drops her oil lamp—the flame goes out, and
they're left in the dark.*)

SCENE THREE: HAPPY NEW YEAR!

M: Totya! (*He clears his throat. He is rehearsing his congratulations out loud…weighing his choice of words—is the tone
right?*) My sweetheart…my dear…my dearest…Anto-
nina Nikolaevna! Totka! My kitten! I wish you…No…I
wish *us* a happy new year! May the year 1942 be completely
different: cheerful and normal. May we live to see another
time…a new time…When we can live well and (*he

*emphasizes the next word*) normally... May you preserve...

T: (*She enters. Her every movement is full of effort, she is covered in snow.*) Okh. I barely had the strength to go out, and barely got myself back up here. I don't want to do aaa-nyyy-thing.

M: My dearest beloved...

T: Don't say that—it's all words, Motya, just words!

M: It's not just words! It's New Year's... We said we would celebrate!

T: Believe me, I know... it's thanks to that miserable New Year's of yours I just walked four hours to get gifts from home... See, I got them. (*She rummages around in her many layers of clothing and eventually finds a small package.*)

M: Which one did you bring?

T: Hold on... not everything at once... Remember, the main thing is the anticipation.

M: Anticipation! Yes, you're really tired and sleepy... but you're still excited... (*The memory perks him up.*)

T: Musenka, how about we go downstairs to the bomb shelter like we were thinking? I mean, you know... there are people... and it seems a little warmer. And there's more light. And maybe they'll give us something to chew. To mark the holiday?

M: But we wanted to celebrate together. Just the two of us. Together. With nobody else around. Downstairs they'll be making big speeches praising the artillery—you know I can't take that anymore.

T: True, we're better off without the war speeches. All right, sweetheart, let me show you what I brought. (*She pulls a little package out of a pocket buried deep inside her clothing; she does this with difficulty, takes a long time unwrapping it—and a silvery sand, dust, falls out.*) Akh!

M: What happened?

T: It's smashed! It's destroyed!

M: Which one was it?

T: (*in a weepy voice*) It was our bullfinch . . . The one we . . .

M: There there, love, it's just a glass bullfinch . . .

T: (*in despair*) But that was Father's bullfinch! I remember we would put it on the Christmas tree together. It was a piece of my childhood, my happiness! There's nothing left of that happiness, just think . . . No more Papa, no more bullfinch . . . I'm such a stupid idiot, slipping on the embankment like that . . .

M: Darling, you fell down? But these things happen! Don't cry . . . (*He awkwardly embraces Totya; he rocks and comforts her, as if he were trying to lull her with his words.*) You know, someone I know told me a very strange story. It's almost impossible to believe. He said he went to the store a few days ago to buy Christmas decorations! Imagine . . . (*Totya keeps sobbing and shaking.*) He said the ridiculous urge remains . . . Those were his exact words, "ridiculous urge"— to buy Christmas decorations. His family—just like yours, Totya—would always put up a bright, colorful Christmas tree, and now decorations belong to his memories and hopes, they're a bridge to the past. So, anyway, in December he and his wife, arm in arm, made it to the store and bought some decorations—a samovar with a teapot and a few other things. The store was semidark, lit by a gas lamp. When they left the toys and went out into the night, they were nearly killed by the cold and the merciless onset of winter. So, Totya, maybe we can buy a bullfinch there . . .

T: (*deflected from her grief over the bullfinch*) Good lord, who's selling them nowadays, those decorations? Why on earth? Who in this dead city would buy them?

M: Well, whoever still remembers some happiness...

T: Now we don't have any presents.

M: I have one for you... (*He goes over to the table, and for a long time he mumbles, fusses, digs around, pulls things out.*) Here it is, sweetheart!

T: (*in disbelief*) What is this? A record?

M: (*with exaggerated cheer*) Yes!

T: But there's no gramophone...

M: Well, yes, that did occur to me... But you know what...

T: What?

M: We'll just remember how it goes! Our music. Here we go...we'll sit ourselves down and start remembering. (*He helps Totya up onto the table and triumphantly sits next to her.*)

(*At first there's an agonizing silence, since there is, of course, no music. But then their somber waltz gradually becomes audible.*)

T: Yes...that's so nice. I remember it now. I remember the entire thing...

M: (*shouting over the waltz*) Dear Comrades! (*Parodying the voice of a radio announcer.*) My dearest Totya! May the New Year be warmer and brighter, may it be normal. May we survive, get *ourselves* back, and live again.

T: Yes, may we live again...live a little longer.

M: Totya, you...are my life. You...are my life.

(*The sound of the music finally overwhelms his voice.*)

## SCENE FOUR: DIARY OF A CAVEMAN. WRITING BY FEEL. JANUARY.

*(Projected on the screen at the back of the stage, excerpts from Moisei's diary appear and disappear (melt away); someone is writing as though he were blind; letters and words crawl on top of each other.)*

M: Antonina, wake up!

T: Oh, don't touch me, really, please don't touch me . . .

M: (*He triumphantly pulls a notebook from deep in his rags.*) Okay, now it's time, time to read you my diary.

T: (*unenthusiastically*) But you can't see anything, Musenka. What is the point? What's the point of the whole thing?

M: Well, I want to do it . . . I want to know what you think! (*He clears his throat. Then he starts declaiming.*) "Diary of a Caveman": Grease burns reliably and has an aromatic scent but casts a terribly dim light—you have to write almost by feel. Today, after crawling out from under the bedclothes before eleven, I spent more than an hour messing around with a new can and wick (a piece of cotton). I got my hands, the matches, and the table all smeared with pomade, but it didn't work—I can't control my hands. We ate breakfast around eleven—I had a dose of cod-liver oil and two tablets of vitamin B, and Tonya had two spoonfuls of pine bark extract. A luxury.

T: Who could possibly be interested in this, Musya—how many spoonfuls of cod-liver oil we had? How much oil cake we stole from each other . . .

M: How can you say that?

T: Okay, or wanted to steal from each other . . . but didn't . . .

we were too ashamed...or didn't have the energy...
It's so squalid...Maybe it would be better if you left
that out?

M: What do you mean, leave it out? It's...what happened!

T: But don't let people know about that...it would be better to leave us out, leave it blank instead of this shame,
this whole shaaame-orgy. Don't let anyone see this horror,
don't let them know! Let it be forgotten, sink to the bottom of the sea.

M: Why? Oh no, I think we must write about everything,
just as it is, Totenka. The truth and nothing but the truth!

T: Somehow I'm not convinced that later on anyone's going
to be too interested in this truth of ours...

M: How can that be? Nobody will want to know? Why not?

T: Well, you know, we aren't the most pleasant spectacle...
average mummies, unsatisfactory condition.

M: Oh ye of little faith! I am sure someone will want to know
about us. So I need to write it down. So that afterwards
their words—I mean, the words of people who come
later—won't be pasted over our words! Over these black
days of ours! So later on nobody can just say whatever
they want about what it was like—afterwards—after we're
gone...

T: What are you saying?

M: You know, afterwards...saying we were all heroes or
villains, or that we suffered beautifully and with honor,
or that we didn't suffer at all...You need to describe
things as they are—the stench, the dark, the improvised
toilet, the abjection, the terror...and you as you are—
sweet, glowing, slender, emaciated...

T: Hah, covered in fleas, starving, vicious...

M: Exactly—the way it is, all the stench, all the boredom,

and then your face—so intelligent, so lovely...every single day, every fact! That's the important thing, just the facts...in full detail—and no whining!

T: Bah!...Boredom, you say!...You won't get bored around here! And who's whining? I'm not a whiner—and you, you're no whiner either. You're my Musya. My Achilles—my worn-out Wellies. With a hole in your rain boot... But I am upset that you're falling down all the time... You definitely have an Achilles' heel...

M: Not all the time, Totenka! Don't exaggerate! Actually, I notice you've been looking for excuses to lose hope!

T: And you, sweetheart, have been looking for excuses to lose your balance—you completely smashed your hip! It's got no moving parts...

M: Totya, you are my moving part! Look, last week I wrote this down specifically: "Today I'm walking fairly well." (*Did you hear that?—I'm walking fair-ly well.*) "Automobiles don't smell like pine trees anymore, more like something artificial—some cloying confectionary smell."

T: What, in fact, could smell like that? Musya, why don't you go ahead and say it—that a truckload of corpses went by...there are almost no other vehicles on the road...

*(Moisei keeps on reading.)*

M: "I got home quickly and only fell once, but walking down the back corridor of the Hermitage, the hall of vases, I went down four times.

"I barely made it to the Academy. Using the tire tracks of passing cars.

"The ice is beautiful covered with frost and smoky mist. Saint Isaac's Cathedral and the sun behind the mist.

"I fell again, in the same place as yesterday, and broke my hand and my hip."

*(Projected on the screen are clips of documentary footage from the blockade, of pedestrians on Nevsky Prospect.*

*Moisei walks along the front of the screen, falls down, gets up, falls down, gets up—and repeats this many times... He stops and, trying to keep his balance, draws in the air with one hand an outline of the city. He reads on.)*

M: "Today I was drawing with one hand, then my hand started to hurt, and I was practically drawing with my nose, since I could barely see. I was tired from the strain of doing the crosshatching, but my mood rose and I got going, until I felt like I was in the saddle again:

"Giddy-up, giddy-up! We're hitting the trail!"

Can you imagine, that's exactly how I wrote it: "Giddy-up, giddy-up! We're hitting the trail!"

*(Moisei tries to hug Totya, to "dance" with her and "play horse." They move sadly and clumsily. In bursts, like the sound of a record skipping, the melody of "The Snow Queen" plays.)*

M: And further on I write: Art is a good thing! Worth living for!

T: It says that? Let me see... Hmm... You really think it's worth it?... A good thing...

M: A good thing!

T: Well, Irakly said: "When I look at Cézanne and then close my eyes, I'm not afraid of anything, I feel lighter." He felt lighter... and then he got ve-e-e-ry light!

M: Really, Antonina, I don't want to know. Don't you dare keep mentioning him.

T: What an idiot. I'm not talking about that. I've forgotten almost everything...everything...I don't remember anything, I don't know anything anymore, Musya. Where did the cigarettes go?

*(They take a long time lighting up, blissfully, like they were kissing, stopping and shaking their heads from pleasure, and from pain: Everything hurts all the time, they're always uncomfortable. Moisei perks up a little and continues "drawing" in the air with his wrapped-up hands: In one of his "paws" is the lit cigarette, and he draws with that. Their movements again resemble a dance, but a dance of dystrophics: Moisei wants to, then he doesn't, then he can, then he can't, expend strength on his "drawings"—it's clear that he hurts all over.)*

T: Moisei, tell me, will it be all right?

M: It will be all right.

T: And what, what could possibly be all right—what the hell are you talking about?

M: Adrian Leonidovich says a new clinic is opening—they're feeding people! They're giving out kasha! And I hear they've even got their own banya...

T: They do, but it's not for the likes of us, Musenka. We're not the ones building tanks. We're useless people. So what are you drawing now?

M: You really can't see?

T: No, not really.

M: How silly you are! Look, here's the embankment,

Petropavlovskaya, the spire hidden in mist as the sun rises and trucks carry the corpses away...

*(Here the most vivid, color images of the city made by blockade artists—Bobyshov, Glebova—can be projected onto the screen.)*

T: I wonder whether they collected ours from the basement. Did a truck take them away, too, I wonder?

M: No, Totenka, I don't think that's worth wondering about... Some say, why even collect them? Why touch them? They look so peaceful, frozen, beautiful...

T: It really is unbelievable! That ass Kontsevich lying there next to Irakly... God, if anyone had told him, with his endless ballerinas and blonds...who he would have to die next to... She even reported on us, the hag, she wrote denunciations about all of us—the old bitch!

M: *(laughing weakly)* Totik, I have to fine you again! You won't get your cigarette tomorrow, and you'll have to listen for hours as I recite Kontsevich's views about the achievements of socialist realism...

T: Is that so! Then I fine you back.

M: There, that's more like it! You sound like the little robber girl again—that's good!

T: There is no more little robber girl... You know, old lady Ganzen, who translated Andersen from Danish, yes, the translator—they say she also... Anna Pavlovna says—it was back in December...They say she burned all her books to stay warm...which means, she even burned "The Snow Queen"...Lit it right up! Hold my hand, little Kay. Hold me.

M: I can't even hold a thought in my head, sweetie...my hands are so frozen...it feels like they're splitting.

*(Totya takes a long time freeing from their coverings a long, elegant, thin, strong hand and places it on Moisei's face.)*

M: Totya . . . my Totya.

*(They are silent. Moisei continues reading.)*

M: "I couldn't move at all. Totya heated up fish oil mixed with the usual pig fat, then put the uncapped oil lamp in the bag. Kerosene spilled everywhere and soaked five packs of cigarettes. We snapped at each other, poor thing! Tonya took refuge on the cot.

"The sight of my sick little girl breaks my heart, and she doesn't understand, she tries to persuade me she just has a cold.

"As far as our condition goes, we've either hit the floor or the ceiling! For the first time, I wasn't so sure we were going to make it . . ."

Tell me . . . Tell me! Tell me it's going to be all right!

*(Totya lies curled into a ball, with her head under the covers. Moisei sits next to her and softly, pleadingly calls/asks/whimpers: "Totya!")*

### SCENE FIVE: BROKEN MIRROR.

M: My beautiful Totya, do you happen to have a mirror?
T: (*peevishly*) What, there aren't enough mirrors in the Hermitage for you, my vain Musya?
M: There used to be all kinds of mirrors, but most of them shattered in the bombings. Do you have a compact?

T: I do not have a compact. I haven't looked at myself in two months. I'm afraid to. I looked once—*mon Dieu*! Bald, blackened, aged... And not even aged but beyond aging... Some kind of, you know, allegorical image of war. Goya.

M: (*preoccupied with something*) But I really, really need a mirror!

T: Well, there are pieces all over the floor. Pick one up and look. Admire yourself.

*(Moisei laboriously seeks out and picks up a shard; he turns it this way and that, trying to look in his mouth, but because his hands are all wrapped up, he has trouble.)*

M: Totya, hold the glass for me! Well, that's what I thought! A third tooth is gone. It's loose, the bastard, and will fall out any minute. Then I'll have another hoooole! Like the holes in Gostiny Dvor...

T: Exactly. And on Pestel, where the bakery was.

M: And Nadezhdinsky. Lidochka lived on that street, your friend. What happened to her?

T: Moisei, how do I know? The phones stopped working back when... No one knows anything about anyone, they can't possibly know and no longer want to. I don't know what happened to my Lidochka. But you know what? Hold that glass up for me, Musya.

M: No.

T: No? Yes!

*(Moisei turns the piece of glass one way, then another, away from Tonya. Light flashes off the mirror in all directions.)*

M: You have such beautiful eyes, such a beautiful forehead, such beautiful hair...You're funny, capricious, golden, you're glowing...

T: Is that true?

M: (*like he's suddenly exhausted*) No, my love. *That is not true.* You have red gums from scurvy, brown skin covered in spots, your eyes are sunken—but you're alive! You're uglier than death itself, my Totya, but you're alive, and that's all that matters now: to survive.

T: Your mirror is crooked and evil! Why should we survive, when we're so horrifying? We can't even look at each other anymore.

M: I know! But, Totya, you couldn't stop looking at me before! You were licking your lips: "My boy, my gorgeous boy." You were telling all of Leningrad about me. You remember last summer, in Komarovo?

T: Oh, I remember last summer. You were running after all the Hermitage queens, including, of course, Lidochka. You were drooling over them, like they were Greek statues. I just bided my time, until you noticed me...

M: Well, they all behaved like Greek statues, I should say. I had absolutely no interest...But you, now, Antonina Nikolaevna, why would I look your way? It was clear you'd mock me for it.

T: (*astonished*) How so?

M: Because you made fun of everyone, Totya. You had such a terrifying, scathing laugh (*he tries to replicate it, but it comes out faint, like a bark*)—ha-ha-ha!

T: (*repeating it just as faintly*) Ha-ha-ha! You once said that no one in the city laughs anymore. There's no laughing during the blockade. The blockade, according to Adrian, has canceled humor... (*Making an effort to liven up, on the strength of her slightly warmed-up vanity.*) So, anyway, how did you finally dare look my way?

M: I dared? Totya, I dared when you, *pardonnez-moi*, undid my shirt...

T: No, you definitely weren't looking my way then—you turned away in horror, innocent Moisei. But my curiosity was piqued!

M: (*indignant*) Your curiosity?

T: I got curious about you—that day when you were the only one, the *only one*, who dared ask that sleazebag Kontsevich at a meeting whether Rembrandt also was a Trotskyite and a formalist, since all the formalists learned from him...

M: You were so curious that you invited me to Komarovo—to pick blueberries.

T: Mmmm, it was so warm and sunny! Remember? I take some berries in my palm...then I put them in your mouth...And my whole palm is in your mouth, and you squash the berries with your tongue and lick my palm... you squash them one by one...and they burst...and juice runs out. Moisei, why are you...fidgeting like that? From the sweet memory? Hard to believe. You haven't laid a finger on me since December...

M: (*sharply*) No, not hard to believe. (*He "unnoticeably" rubs at his cap with a bound hand.*)

T: What's wrong?...Oh...You have lice, my love?

M: Antonina Nikolaevna, how can you speak like that to me! Leave me alone!

T: Dear God, what's the problem—we all have lice. The living have lice, and the dead, too. If there's one thing that unites us during the blockade, it's that. They bite at Party headquarters, and they bite us here in our basement. Sweetheart, let me take your cap off and have a look.

M: Don't you dare! I have ... I have hives.

T: Moisei, you blockhead. It's not hives ... Allow me to unmask you. (*Playfully*) *Komm zu mir* ... (*Moisei whimpers unhappily but doesn't really object.*) There it is, my dear—now let me grab it: easy now, easy ...

M: Disgusting ...

T: Why disgusting? Just a raised white spot with a dot in the middle!

M: So disgusting!

T: You know, it occurs to me that blockade lice may be the essence of blockade love.

M: How can you say that? Disgusting!

T: I think it's true. Lice are very weak and very firm. Nothing gets rid of them. Nits, now—they're the best. They're like berries, like blueberries—I would pull them off slowly-slowly, gently-gently, and you would watch and watch. And I would watch you watching. (*Totya stands over Moisei and searches in his hair. They are illuminated in a small, weak cone of light.*) Moisei, you are so handsome! You have such beautiful hair, a beautiful forehead, beautiful everything. Just everything.

SCENE SIX: THE SNOW QUEEN. FEBRUARY.

(*Darkness. The radio plays: triumphant news reports.*)

T: Moisei, get up! (*starts coughing*) Get up! Bring my coffee!

Cut the games, please! (*Raising her voice in an annoyed monotone.*) Moisei, time to get up! You need to stop faking! Get up already!

M: I'm not feeling so good...today. I don't think...don't think I can...

T: It's all in your head...Why do you always invent things? You do it all the time! You're indulging yourself....This alleged weakness of yours—it's self-indulgence! I'm sick and tired of your helplessness! Why can't you do anything?

M: Don't...don't do that...you have to stop!

T: Why can't you do anything?

M: I, yes...I'm getting up...See: I'm getting up! (*With agonizing, long, slow effort, he gets up, goes over to get the pot, tries to pick it up with his wrapped-up hands—and, of course, he drops it, very loudly, and water goes everywhere.*)

T: (*gives a piercing shriek*) Aaaaaaa! You idiot! Why do you always have to make a mess!

M: Don't do that! (*He holds his hands to his head, shielding himself from her voice.*)

T: (*shrieking hysterically*) I can't take it anymore...I can't stand you...I just can't! You keep making a mess!

M: Are you all right, Totenka?

(*Here Totya should turn into the Snow Queen, while the coldest, loudest, most terrifying version of her song plays. For example: Totya climbs up onto the table, "gets bigger," in her white bedclothes, lit by white and blue light. Moisei's voice— not his blockade voice but a very beautiful, strong, steady, velvety voice—reads from above/behind the stage.*)

M's VOICE: There stood a tall, statuesque, blindingly white

woman—the Snow Queen; she was wearing a fur coat and a hat made of snow.

"Are you still freezing?" she asked, and kissed him on the forehead.

Oh! Her kiss was colder than ice; its cold pierced him all over and went to his very heart, which was already half frozen. For a second Kay thought he was going to die, but on the contrary, he started feeling better and even stopped feeling cold.

"I won't kiss you anymore!" she said. "Or I'll kiss you to death!"

Kay looked at her: She was so beautiful! He couldn't imagine a more intelligent, charming face. She didn't seem like ice anymore, like she did when she sat outside his window and nodded her head to him; now she seemed like perfection.

M: (*Lying on the floor next to the empty coffeepot.*) Totya! (*He tries to be heard over the music.*) Don't, you're going to kill me!...Don't torture me! I'm cold! I'm cold! Please forgive me! (*He cries.*) I'm an idiot, I know it's hard being with me, it's so hard for you...My poor, poor girl... My...little one...you're tired!

(*Here they can speak at the same time, shouting and whispering, not listening to one another, like lovers singing their aria-duets in an opera, except there's no harmony, just a nightmarish mutual non-hearing.*)

T: (*in an icy voice*) Oh, this is unbearable! Unbearable! When is this going to end? I can't listen to you anymore...Your complaints! Your demands! (*Suddenly her hysterics inexplicably "freeze," and Totya shifts to a totally calm voice.*) I don't care anymore...Do you understand...Moisei. Nothing matters anymore. May it end as soon as possible... as soon as possible!

*(Carrying the same small lamp as she did earlier, Anna Pav-lovna enters very slowly. She has changed drastically: In place of the lively, high-strung woman, we see an aged shadow, and she can only whisper due to her scurvy.)*

AP: Moisei Borisovich! Moisei Borisovich! Moisei Borisov-ich! There's wonderful news, just wonderful—you're ad-mitted to the clinic. They're going to help you, they have kaa-shaa, they've got heat, they save everyone...everyone there will be saved! *(She slowly walks downstage, then stops still and quietly "falls asleep"—behind her, a sheet of white paper falls, swirling.)*

T: *(Coming back to herself, she gets down from her "pedestal," abandoning the role of Snow Queen/Blockade Death, and crawls over to the piece of paper—a notice of admission to the clinic. She cries out.)* Musya, it's...Can it be?! The clinic!

M: Don't...

T: They finally came through with admission to the clinic... Now you don't have to die!

M: Don't...

T: You're going to the clinic right this minute...They finally understood...that you're a brilliant boy...and you can't be allowed to freeze!

M: For the love of God...Leave me alone...Don't touch me, don't torture me! I'm not going anywhere now...

T: *(Lowers herself onto the floor next to him.)* You're going! You are going! You won't die here! You know it can't end like this—you know it's just the beginning, right? Look, I'm sorry. But you need to get up! Get up! (*Moisei clings to her knees, and we can see her face; their poses replicate the composition of Rembrandt's* Prodigal Son.) You're going to go, you're going to eat, they are going to feed you, they are going to bathe you, they will heal your hands, you'll draw the whole thing for them...you'll fucking show them this hell of ours...You'll explain everything to them. Remember, Tyrsa said you're a brilliant boy, with a promising future. You'll realize that promise, won't you, Musya? Come on, get up, good, my strong boy! You heard what she said: Everyone there will be saved.

(*Moisei leans on Totya, gets up, and slowly moves toward the exit; he keeps looking back at Totya with fear, hope, and the semblance of an encouraging smile—but it's a gruesome smile.*)

T: Go on! Go...It's warm there, it's bright! Musya...Go!

(*A triumphant blockade newscast plays on the radio. We hear some interference, and then Totya's voice, with precise enunciation, like the voice of an announcer.*)

T's VOICE: Moisei Vakser died at the aid station on February 4, 1942. Totya, Antonina Izergina, was not at his side that night. Most of his unpublished works, letters, and photographs have not been found.

(*Paintings by Moisei Vakser are projected onto the screen, one by one. Cue the music.*)

# NOTES

EASTSTRANGEMENT

5 *go to Victory Park:* Victory Park is a large recreational park in Saint Petersburg.

6 *the dystrophics:* During the siege, Leningraders who showed symptoms of starvation were called "dystrophics."

7 *Kosheverova's* Cinderella*:* Soviet filmmaker Nadezhda Kosheverova (1902–1989) specialized in children's films. Her highly regarded film *Cinderella* (1947) was written by Evgeny Shvarts and starred Faina Ranevskaia and Yanina Zheimo.

*Akhmatova's courtyard...courtyard of Berggolts*: Anna Akhmatova (1889–1966) was a major twentieth-century poet whose career spanned the prerevolutionary and Soviet periods. Olga Berggolts (1910–1975) was a Soviet poet and Party member who was most famous for her radio broadcasts during the Siege of Leningrad.

8 *Georgy "the Matador" Makogonenko* (1912–1986) was an important Soviet literary scholar.

9 *Tanya Savicheva's diary:* Tanya Savicheva (1930–1944), whose entire family died during the siege, wrote the best-known siege diary by a schoolgirl.

*Piskaryovskoe Cemetery:* The site of an official Soviet memorial to victims of the siege.

10 *performed the Seventh Symphony:* Composed by Dmitry Shostakovich (1906–1975) after the Germans invaded Russia and laid siege to Leningrad. It is popularly known as the "Leningrad Symphony."

11 *the conductor Eliasberg's hands:* Karl Eliasberg (1907–1978) was the conductor of the Leningrad Radio Orchestra.

THE FORGIVER

In this essay, Barskova speaks as a scholar who has done archival research on the Siege of Leningrad. The central figure is Dmitry Maximov (1904–1987), a professor at Leningrad University who taught prerevolutionary literature to Soviet students. He was best known for his studies of Alexander Blok (1880–1921), Russia's finest symbolist poet. Less publicly, Maximov was a survivor of the siege and the author of poetry about the experience.

The other key figure is Barskova's birth father, Evgeny Rein. Along with Joseph Brodsky (1940–1996), Rein was one of "Akhmatova's orphans," a group of young Petersburg poets who began writing during the post-Stalin period without regard for Soviet censorship. Rein lives in Russia and remains a respected literary figure.

13　*"Behold: the hawk prepares his strength":* From Blok's long poem "Retribution" (1921).

14　*Klodt's famous horses:* Peter Clodt von Jürgensburg (known in Russia as Pyotr Klodt, 1805–1867) was the sculptor who created the equestrian statues *The Horse Tamers* on Anichkov Bridge in Saint Petersburg.

15　*"No one is forgotten":* A line of poetry by Olga Berggolts, inscribed on the monument in Piskaryovskoe Cemetery.

18　*the Italian Jew Primo Levi:* Primo Levi (1919–1987) was a scientist and a writer. An Italian of Jewish descent, he was deported to Auschwitz during World War II, and his most famous books document that experience.

22　*"the pseudonym Ignaty Karamov":* Maximov's poetry was published abroad under the pseudonym Ignaty Karamov. This kind of publishing—known as *tamizdat*, or "publishing over there"—was practiced in the late Soviet period. Manuscripts were smuggled out of the country and published in different countries, not always with the author's permission and review.

23　*unceasing anguish of ivan ilyich:* A reference to Leo Tolstoy's story "The Death of Ivan Ilyich."

26　*IL PADRE TUO!:* A phrase from the libretto of Giuseppe Verdi's *Luisa Miller.*

28　*Maximov—Zaltsman—Gor—Voltman—Spasskaya—Krandievskaya-Tolstaya—Gnedich:* The names of writers who survived the siege and whose poetry about the experience could not be published during the Soviet era.

A GALLERY

This "gallery" features three painters: Pablo Picasso is the hero of the first piece; a painting by J. M. W. Turner figures in the second; and an exhibit of Arshile Gorky's work plays a role in the third piece, about Barskova's naturalization ceremony in Lowell, Massachusetts.

34 *the mysterious hole's contents:* A reference to Guillaume Apollinaire, who received a head wound during World War I, which eventually killed him.

39 *Arsène Lupin or D.:* Arsène Lupin is the hero of a detective series written by the French novelist Maurice Leblanc. "D." refers to Edgar Allan Poe's detective character C. Auguste Dupin in "The Murders in the Rue Morgue," "The Mystery of Marie Rogêt," and "The Purloined Letter."

40 *Memorial Auditorium:* A historic building in Lowell, Massachusetts, where new US citizens are sworn in.

*I tried to imagine:* Efim Etkind (1918–1999) was a Soviet scholar and dissident who emigrated to France. Mikhail Lozinsky (1886–1955) was a celebrated translator of Shakespeare, among other authors.

42 *that same rat's tail:* The pawnbroker in Dostoyevsky's *Crime and Punishment* has such a "rat's tail."

43 *Obvodny Canal:* The canal borders an industrial area of Saint Petersburg, where factories such as Red Triangle were located.

45 *suggestive name ("Bitter"):* The name Gorky means bitter, which is why Maxim Gorky (1868–1936), the writer and communist intellectual, took it as a revolutionary surname. (His real name was Alexei Peshkov.) The word "bitter" is traditionally pronounced at wedding feasts to prompt the newlyweds to kiss.

MODERN TALKING

The setting is a Soviet summer camp for Pioneers, a Party-sponsored children's organization, something like the American Scouts but with an explicit ideological program. However, these camps were open to all and were frequented by children whose families did not own summer homes, or dachas. Different camps were funded by different institutions; Barskova's was run by the KGB, as the governing entity at her stepfather's place of employment.

47 *the pedantic Kun:* Nikolai Kun (1877–1940) is best known as the author of *Legends and Myths of Ancient Greece*, which has been continuously in print since its first appearance in 1922.

49 *Modern Talking:* A male pop duo from Germany that became internationally popular during the mid-1980s with their hit "You're My Heart, You're My Soul."

50 *Somov's marquises:* Konstantin Somov (1869–1939) was a painter associated with Russian turn-of-the-century ornamental and decadent art. He created the illustrations for censored editions, in German, French, and Russian, of *The Book of the Marquises,* a collection of eighteenth-century erotic texts by authors such as André Chénier, Giacomo Casanova, Pierre Choderlos de Laclos, and others.

*"And the watchmen draw":* A line from Alexander Pushkin's *The Little Tragedies.*

## ULIANOVA IN AUGUST

Soviet literature for young adults abounded in books about Vladimir Ilyich Lenin, whose actual surname was Ulianov. In this family reminiscence, the young Barskova unfavorably compares her own family to the perfectly happy Ulianovs and identifies with Lenin's sister Olga Ulianova, named in the essay's title.

54 *named for the geographer:* Peter Kropotkin (1842–1921) was an influential anarchist and revolutionary activist who was arrested and exiled by the tsarist regime. He trained as a scientist while serving in the imperial army in his youth and made some important contributions to the study of geology.

*the Fortress:* The Peter and Paul Fortress in Saint Petersburg.

55 *The librarian:* Nadezhda Krupskaia (1869–1939), a Bolshevik and Lenin's wife, suffered from Basedow's disease, also known as Graves' disease.

56 *Bonch-Bruevich … saffron-colored elf*: Vladimir Bonch-Bruevich, Sigizmund Krzhizhanovsky, Lidia Polezhaeva, and Zoya Voskrensenskaya all wrote books for Soviet children, as did the "saffron-colored elf," Mikhail Zoshchenko, best known for his satirical writings. During World War II he was evacuated from Leningrad to Almaty, Kazakhstan.

*"What a close family we were":* Maria Alexandrovna and Ilya Nikolaevich are the names and patronymics of Lenin's parents.

*The march to the scaffold:* Lenin's older brother, Alexander Ulianov, was executed in 1887 after his participation in a failed assassination attempt against Alexander III.

BROTHERS AND THE BROTHERS DRUSKIN

Of the two Druskin brothers, Yakov Druskin (1902–1980) was the more significant for Russian literature. He was a philosopher and musician associated with OBERIU, a group of avant-garde intellectuals which met in the early 1930s. This group included the writer Daniil Kharms (1905–1942), whose manuscripts Druskin saved after Kharms died in a prison psychiatric ward during the Siege of Leningrad. Druskin's brother, Mikhail (1905–1991), was a concert pianist and musicologist who taught at the Leningrad Conservatory.

63 *He would report to Sollertinsky:* Ivan Sollertinsky (1902–1944) was a musicologist, professor at the Leningrad Conservatory, and artistic director of the Leningrad Symphony Orchestra.
*Mikhail looks at Shostakovich:* Dmitry Shostakovich, a Soviet-era composer of international fame.

66 *Venezuelan exile Marina Durnovo:* Marina Durnovo (née Malich, 1912–2002) was Kharms's second wife, who later emigrated to Venezuela. Her remarkable life story is featured in the essay "Hair Sticks."

PERSEPHONE'S GROVE

This piece takes the reader beyond Russia to Barskova's émigré life in San Francisco in the 2000s. The distance of emigration allows a meditation on ethical-sexual mores in the late Soviet period.

69 *The Herzog:* The Duc de Blangis, who is a central character in the Marquis de Sade's *The 120 Days of Sodom.* (In Russian and German, the title Herzog is equivalent to Duke.)

76 *Once again I visited:* The opening words of a famous poem by Pushkin.

78 *my totsky/myshkin, my frigid nastasia:* Characters from Dostoyevsky's *The Idiot.*

79 *countless Justines or Eugenies:* Justine is the eponymous heroine of the Marquis de Sade's novella *Justine, or the Misfortunes of Virtue,* and Eugenie is the heroine of his short story "Eugenie de Franval."

HAIR STICKS

This essay is set in the early years of Barskova's emigration, with a focus on women's experiences. It features the story of Marina Malich, Kharms's second wife. After Kharms died during the siege, Malich crossed the front lines and worked as a laborer in Germany, eventually emigrating to Venezuela.

82 *the book I was carrying around:* Vladimir Glotser's *Marina Durnovo: My Husband Daniil Kharms* (2005) consists of interviews Glotser conducted with Durnovo near the end of her life. (Durnovo was her last husband's surname; Barskova refers to her by her maiden name, Malich.)

84 *story about Little Khavroshechka:* "Little Khavroshechka" is a Russian folktale about a Cinderella-like figure, an orphan girl adopted by a family with three malicious daughters who have, respectively, one, two, and three eyes. The Cyclops in Book 9 of Homer's *Odyssey* has one eye.

85 *flooded by brown waters:* In 2002, Prague experienced its worst flood in five hundred years.

   *disintegrated like the Snow Maiden:* The Snow Maiden (Snegurochka) is a character from Russian folklore who is made of snow. Her girlfriends invite her to play a game in which they jump over a fire, and when the Snow Maiden takes her turn, she evaporates.

## SESTRORETSK, KOMAROVO

The title names two traditional resort areas for the Russian, later Soviet, intelligentsia. Barskova and her father were allowed to visit these state sanatoriums due to his ill health. As she makes clear, standards of care and nutrition at these institutions were not high.

87 *"a railroad prose":* This remark is taken from near the end of Osip Mandelstam's "The Egyptian Stamp."

90 *or Panova:* Vera Panova (1905–1973), a Leningrad prose writer and dramaturge.

91 *It's a woman speaking:* Akhmatova, who in her later years kept a dacha in Komarovo, where she is buried. Komarovo was annexed from Finland after World War II and developed as a vacation spot for the Soviet intelligentsia.

   *Dumas père:* Alexandre Dumas père (1802–1870), a famously prolific French novelist.

92 *The unknown passionate sinologist:* Boris Vakhtin (1930–1981) was a distinguished sinologist and nonconformist writer. He was Panova's son and is buried next to her in the Komarovo cemetery.

## DONA FLOR AND HER GRANDMOTHER

Reminiscences of time spent with Barskova's mother's family in Siberia—as a young child, and as a teenager whose older lover was killed in a pedestrian accident on Nevsky Prospect in Leningrad.

97 *Forty years ago an aged Anaïs Nin:* Anaïs Nin (1903–1977), the author of works in French, Spanish, and English, is most famous for her erotica and her diary. She was a guest at the founding ceremony of Hampshire College, where Barskova taught for more than a decade.

99 *that's what Bunin would have called them:* Ivan Bunin (1870–1953) was the first Russian writer to win the Nobel Prize in Literature. He was a close friend of Anton Chekhov (1860–1904) during Chekhov's last years, before he succumbed to tuberculosis. Chekhov married Olga Knipper, a principal actor with the Moscow Art Theater, in 1901.

100 *a certain devotee of words and sounds:* Refers to Vladimir Nabokov (1899–1977).

103 *Joe Dassin was floating:* Joe Dassin (1938–1980) was a singer popular in France in the 1960s and '70s. Barskova refers to his song "Et si tu n'existais pas."

## REAPER OF LEAVES

The writer Vitaly Valentinovich Bianki (1894–1959) was beloved by many generations for his children's stories. His best-known work is his column "The Forest Newspaper," originally published in the children's magazine *The New Robinson*, where he "reported" on events in the natural world. He was arrested many times by the Soviet authorities but survived the Stalin era. He visited Leningrad during the siege and left a valuable record of what he observed.

The other hero of the piece is Evgeny Shvarts (1896–1958), who wrote for theater and film, and also for children, like many of his unpublishable friends among the OBERIU. He also kept a voluminous record of Leningrad literary life. (He once said, "I write everything, except denunciations.") Before he was evacuated from besieged Leningrad in December 1941, he wrote anti-Hitler broadcasts for Leningrad Radio and volunteered as a lookout for bombing raids.

107 *Bianki grabbed me by the legs:* An excerpt from Shvarts's notebooks.

109 *Like all the jokesters:* Shvarts, Kharms, and other OBERIU members wrote for the children's magazines *The Hedgehog* (published 1928–1935) and *The Siskin* (published 1930–1941).

110 *A young boy...passes dioramas*: Bianki's father, Valentin Bianki, was an ornithologist who worked in the zoological section of the Academy of Sciences Museum.

114 *Socialist Revolutionaries:* The Socialist Revolutionary Party played a central role in the overthrow of the tsarist regime. After the October Revolution, many SRs (as members of the party were called) opposed Bolshevik rule and were persecuted.

115 *E. P. Peshkova's intervention:* Ekaterina Peshkova (1876–1965) was Maxim Gorky's first wife. She became an important human rights activist, helping to found the Political Red Cross, which aided political prisoners until it was shut down in 1937.

120 *his failed play:* Shvarts's unfinished play was titled *Blockade Night* (1943).

*hatred-passion for Oleinikov:* Nikolai Oleinikov (1898–1937) was a poet and one of the OBERIUs. As the editor of *The Hedgehog* and *The Siskin*, he was responsible for bringing them in as contributors.

121 *Voevodins, Rysses, and Azarovs:* Minor representatives of official Leningrad literature.

## LIVING PICTURES

Barskova created the genre term "fairy-tale document" for her first play, which premiered in 2016 at the Theater of the Nation in Moscow and remains in its repertoire. The fairy tale in question is Hans Christian Andersen's story "The Snow Queen." The document is the archival record of this historical scene: two lovers holed up in the Hermitage Museum during the worst period of the Siege of Leningrad, the autumn and winter of 1941–1942. They were Antonina Izergina (1906–1969), a notable art historian who was the director of the Western European Art section of the Hermitage, and Moisei Vakser (1916–1942), a painter and illustrator, who also made propaganda supporting the Soviet defense against the Germans.

During the siege, employees of the museum lived in its cellars, since communal living was assumed to be more beneficial than remaining in cold, dark individual apartments, and safer than traveling to and from the museum during continual air raids. However, museum staff were not eligible for the state-controlled rations available to what we might call today "essential workers." Dozens of museum staff died of starvation, and their frozen corpses were stored in a room at the Hermitage. It was only in late winter that city authorities managed to establish aid stations where victims of dystrophy were fed.

The Hermitage collections fared better than the staff—much of the art was evacuated to the Far East, leaving empty frames throughout the galleries. As curators testified in their memoirs, staff would give "tours" of the empty frames to sailors who compensated them with food from their state rations.

131 *Ganzen's translation:* Anna Ganzen (1869–1942) was a distinguished translator of Scandinavian literature. Along with her husband, Peter Ganzen, she translated the complete works of Hans Christian Andersen, among other authors. As the head of the Leningrad chapter of the Union of Writers, she remained in Leningrad during the siege and died there.

138 *Orbeli sent her off:* Joseph Orbeli (1887–1961) was a scholar of Eastern studies, member of the Academy of Sciences, and director of the Hermitage Museum from 1934 to 1951. He remained in Leningrad during the siege.

142 *Snyders:* A poem by the literary scholar Lev Pumpiansky (1891–1940).

143 *Roo-roo:* A poem by the artist and writer Pavel Zaltsman (1912–1985).
    *SCENE THREE:* This scene begins with a New Year's greeting but also contains references to Christmas trees and gifts. Initially the Soviets banned Christmas, which, however, remained a popular holiday. In 1935, it was ruled that Christmas would be merged with the secular New Year's holiday.

152 *Bobyshov, Glebova:* Mikhail Bobyshov (1885–1964) was a painter and theater designer. Tatiana Glebova (1900–1985) was an artist and friend of the OBERIUs.

# OTHER NEW YORK REVIEW CLASSICS

*For a complete list of titles, visit www.nyrb.com.*